To err is human. To forgive, K-9.

Sargent Prozak

K-9 PROZAK

POW

RADA JONES

APOLODOR

APOLODOR PUBLISHING

K-9 PROZAK

1

My time's up.

For weeks now, the stars have juggled, shaking up things here in camp, in the scorching Kandahar desert and all over the world. My star just dropped into place, and I know that my life is about to end.

How? I just do. Like I know when I'm thirsty, hungry, or need to poop. Like I know that Rambo, in the crate next to mine, dreams about home. He always smells guilty when he does. Like I know that Cho, my handler, is curled in her cot at the other end of the hangar but she's not asleep. She's brooding with worry. Like I know that the soldiers snoring in their cots are dreaming of their homes. But they're far away. All we have here is the orange desert's scorching heat, the stench of gunpowder and fear, and the never-ending hate.

It's like a smell, but it's not in your nose. It spreads throughout your body. It's like when you're cold — it gets into your bones, and you don't need to see snow to know it.

Do I mind my life being over? A little bit. I'll miss Rambo — the Dutch is a nice pup, always willing to help. And I'll miss the soldiers. They're good folks and mean well, even if they're armed to the teeth and terrified of blowing up. The poor kids are way too young to live in fear. Some are just 18, for Dog's sake. Yeah, I know I'm only seven, but mine are dog years, so each one counts like eight human years. That makes me what? 72? 63? I dunno; I've never been good at math. I should ask Rambo. He's a shepherd, and they start counting in their mother's womb. He can count with his eyes closed and a paw tied behind his back.

Not me. I can count up to five exciting things, like biscuits, balls, begging strips, and bones — but no further. I've always been more interested in what makes people tick. Why do dogs bury their bones? Why do cats wag their tails when they're mad? Why do humans do the things they do instead of whatever makes sense or what's easy? But a lifetime wouldn't be enough for that, and I don't have a lifetime. Things are about to get hairy, so I'd better rest for my last mission.

I curl on my left side and stick my nose under my tail to catch a nap. Tomorrow's gonna be rough, so I'd better be ready. At my age, I need all the sleep I can get. It's bad enough that I have a bad hip and my back gives me trouble. I don't need a foggy brain to top that.

I sigh and close my eyes, looking for a nap, but my skin prickles all over and my hackles go up. I've waited too long.

Heartbeats later, the alarm howls, shattering the desert's silence, and the lights turn on. Two dozen sleepy men jump to their feet, raising the dust from the plywood floors to the corrugated ceiling. They pull on their bulletproof vests and grab their weapons, then run to fight the attack. But we're not under attack. We're under orders, the lieutenant says.

"Listen, everyone. Tonight, we have a special mission. We must find the massive cache of weapons and ammunition the Taliban gathered to fuel their much-touted spring offensive. We'll start before dawn. We'll drive into the mountains, then continue on foot from there. Prozak and Cho are in the lead tonight, and Rambo and Ash will bring up the rear. Everyone else, you know your place. Any questions?"

"Yep. Why us?" Emil asks, scratching his gray stubble. He's

older than the rest, and he always has something to say. That's why the lieutenant loves him like a thorn in his side.

"Because our orders say so. We are the closest unit to that cache, so we're set to go."

"But that's not our kind of mission! We're not special-ops ninjas; we're just a remote K-9 unit guarding the darned desert to prevent the Taliban from taking over. Our strength is our base. We aren't safe anywhere else. And you want us to leave the safety of the wire and drive into the mountains? We may as well paint a target on our backs. Thanks to their informers, the enemy knows where we are and what we're doing just as well as we do. They'll make sure we don't make it to their weapons. Or at least we don't make it back. This sounds like a suicide mission if I ever saw one."

The lieutenant's face twists as if he's trying to bite his ear, like it always does when he's angry. But he misses. No wonder. Even I can't bite my ears, and mine are soft and floppy, not round and stuck to the head like his. The only one who can do it is Lovely, but she's a springer, so she's got pancake ears hanging to her shoulders. The lieutenant doesn't stand a chance.

"As I said, we have orders. This is the army, remember? We do what we're told. We were told to find that cache, and that's precisely what we'll do. Any other questions?"

"What do we do when we find it?" Dan asks.

That poor kid. He struggles with his acne and his fear, but he always tries to do the right thing. And he loves dogs. He always slips me a bit of his MREs when he thinks no one's watching. He hopes to be a dog handler someday.

"I'll let you know, when necessary," the lieutenant spits, and Dan shrinks into his helmet like a snail.

"Let's go," the lieutenant says.

The chaos starts.

2

Wherever we're going, it's not close. We drive half the night, dropping from pothole to pothole and breathing in the gasoline fumes. We're still driving when the black sky bruises to purple before catching fire. A bloody sun rises behind the jagged black mountains, and my heart skips a beat. Something in those fang-like peaks biting the sun tells me that whatever fate awaits me, it won't be good.

I don't know how bad it's gonna get, and I don't really want to. You must think you have a chance to put up a good fight; otherwise, what's the point? I'd rather hang on to hope than know what's coming, even though the smell of danger dries my mouth and tightens my belly.

Oh, well. It is what it is. I'd better check on the others.

To my left, Rambo leans against my shoulder, dressed in a bulletproof vest just like mine. He lays his dark nose on his paws like he's asleep, but his hackles are up, and his sharp ears quiver like antennae. He's scared too, and that's no wonder. The poor kid has never seen a mission like this.

I lick his nose.

"It's OK, Rambo. The sunrise is red. So what? We're in the

desert; they're all red. We just don't get to see them since we're inside. A red sunrise doesn't mean anything here."

His heart slows down. He sighs.

"You're right, Zak. Thanks. This sunrise is just like any other, and we're on a mission like all the others. We'll be back."

I shake my head. I'd love to help him, but I can't lie to him. Especially not today, the last time I see him.

"You'll be back, Ram. But I won't. That's it for me. This is my last mission."

Rambo's heart drums like crazy. He jumps to his feet and sniffs my tail. He's got a hundred questions, but the truck screeches to a stop.

We arrive. Stumbling under the weight of their equipment, the men jump off one after the other, thumping as they hit the ground. Ash, Rambo's trainer, jumps too, and Rambo follows.

It's Cho's turn, but instead of following Ash, she turns to me. The crease between her eyebrows is sharper than ever, and her narrow eyes are heavy with worry.

It's her last mission too, and she knows it.

"How are you doing, Prozak?"

I wag my tail left. That's what we dogs do when things aren't jelling.

"As well as you'd expect. How about you, Cho?"

She glances at the mountain and shakes her head.

"You know, Prozak, I wish I didn't have to do this. Or at least I wish we weren't in the lead."

I cock my head.

"But if it wasn't us, it would be Rambo and Ash. I'm old, and I've lived a whole life, but Ram? He's just starting. I'm glad it's me."

Cho sighs. I try to lick her hand to make her better, but she pulls it away.

The men are waiting.

"Common, Cho. Let's get going, shall we?" the lieutenant says.

Cho jumps off, and I follow.

The first thing I notice is the smell. Now that my nose is no longer jammed by the BO of the soldiers, complete with weapons and ammunition plus the truck's stinky fumes, I breathe the scent of the mountains. The air is cool and thin. It smells like evergreens, with a hint of wood smoke and goat manure. But nothing compares to the omnipresent stench of hate.

Hatred is easy to recognize but hard to describe. It's heavy and visceral, but not in a warm, poop-like sort of way. It's like a cross between the spray of an angry skunk, the tension before a storm, and the putrid stench of rotting garbage. And dead rat. Either way, it's foul and penetrates everything, like hate does. I feel it not only in my nose but in my bones and in my heart.

We all do. Even the men. They carry it inside them, whether they know it or not. Most don't, since the humans' sense of smell is so weak they can't find their own socks or know when someone's lying. The humans' noses seem to have no other purpose but to hold up their glasses. And still, hate poisons us all.

"Let's go."

The lieutenant points to a narrow goat path climbing up the abrupt slope, and I get going. I smell my way up the trail, checking for IEDs, explosives, or anything that could hurt our men. I sniff every rock and check every bush before moving on.

Her eyes down, her hands clutching at rocks and roots to stay upright, Cho follows. She clips her thirty-foot lead to my collar, as usual, so I feel her even though she's far behind. They say thoughts and feelings travel down the leash, and they're right. I can feel Cho's heart beat like crazy and hear her ragged breath.

Way behind, the men follow, stepping in each other's footsteps. Rambo and Ash bring up the rear. Their eyes are peeled for a trap because we all know, even the humans, that that's what this mission is: a trap. Even the lieutenant knows it, though he won't say it. We all feel the noose waiting to close. But if we're very lucky and very smart, we might escape. Maybe.

A murder of crows quarrels up in the canopy. I wonder what

they fight about, but I don't have time to check. I need to focus on this darn trail that's getting harder and harder. I sink my claws into the soft green moss to keep my footing. Cho struggles too. She pulls back on the lead to steady herself, which surely doesn't help, but I do my best to pull her up.

Once in a while, we pass a cleft in the mountain, and I don't like that one bit. The morning sun hits my eyes, so I can't see anything inside the clefts. My hackles go up. It's like there's someone in there watching me. Is it the smell, I wonder? This place stinks like smoke, fear, and hate, just like the Afghan homes. But nothing happens, so I trudge on, wondering how much farther.

Far behind, someone barks.

"Hey, Zak! Take it easy, will you? You wouldn't want to mess your orange do."

That's Rambo. He's kidding, of course. In his roundabout way, he's telling me to take care. Good to know he's watching my back, even though he's too far to help if danger strikes. When it strikes, that is.

"You too, striped warrior," I bark, making fun of his brindle coat. That's the only thing Rambo ever brags about. He loves his coat like it's his flag. Dutch shepherds have to be brindle, so, to him, it's breed and country rolled into one.

Up and up, I keep going.

Cho pants behind me and pulls on the lead more and more. She isn't much into the outdoors, so this is hard for her, but she does the best she can.

The air gets thinner up here. It's cooler, too, though the sun's halfway up the sky and beats on us like a stick. My twisted shadow has grown so long it's already halfway up the ridge. I follow it, pricking my ears to the sounds of the mountain.

Then it hits me. There are no other sounds but ours: the gravel screeching underfoot, the soldiers' heavy breathing, the soft curses when someone's boot slips, the metal sharply clanging against metal.

All else is gone. The crows have gone quiet. The wind has stopped gusting. The trees have stopped moaning. The whole mountain is as silent as a cemetery.

Why?

I lift my muzzle to sniff the air, and the stench of hate chokes me. Where is it coming from, I wonder? I check high and low, but it's everywhere.

All of a sudden, I catch a whiff of something new. And odd.

What's that? And where is it?

I follow my nose to locate it, and I notice the cave.

3

———————

The sun burns my eyes, so I see nothing but darkness. There's no movement, no sound, nothing but a terrible feeling of doom. But it hits me so hard that I sit to warn Cho.

But she's not watching me. She's struggling to crawl over the massive boulder blocking the trail. That thing is stuck in the worst possible spot, just where the trail narrows to a footpath edged by cliffs. I wonder if it's there on purpose.

Way down behind Cho, the men scramble to climb. They pant and curse as they slip over the shifty gravel that rolls under their feet. Their boots may be great in the desert, but not here, where bare rock gives way to rolling gravel and treacherous stones shift under their step. But the men don't relent. They push on, fighting their way up the trail behind Cho.

I'm aghast.

My whole body, from the top of my nose to the tip of my tail, shivers to warn me that something is wrong. I know it, even though the odor I'm getting isn't one of those I've learned. This isn't TNT, black powder, fertilizer, or even RDX. It's some chemical I've never sniffed before, but I know it's bad.

I stare at Cho and will her to stop, but she's not looking at me.

That's nothing new. Cho's always been locked in her bubble, no matter how I've tried to reach her. It's like she's forgotten we are a team, and that's how she's always been.

I first met Cho when they transferred me to the army. I had worked with the border patrol; then I had a stint with law enforcement. But when the Afghan war heated up and they needed more bodies, they sent me here to sniff for IEDs.

I wasn't pleased, since I'd been happy working in Topeka. But my handler retired, and they got rid of me too. They shipped me to Kandahar, where I met Cho.

She was small and thin and she smelled worried. And she hated touching me.

Too bad, I thought, since I always loved being close to my humans. I love belly rubs and tail scratches and even pats on the head, but I knew I'd have to do without them. Cho's brows furrowed, and her eyes narrowed as I sniffed her. She smelled like she didn't want me near.

She stepped back. The old lieutenant frowned.

"This is Prozak. He's a seven-year-old golden retriever, and he's done it all. He's worked with border patrol, law enforcement, and more. He can sniff anything, from bombs to bananas. You'll never find a better K-9, and you're fortunate to have him. You'd better treat him right."

I could tell he didn't like her, though I didn't know why. But that's humans for you. There's no telling as to why they do what they do.

That's how Cho and I started. Now, we've been together for months, but things haven't gotten any better. She still smells like she's doomed, and she avoids touching me.

I gave her space, though it wasn't easy. My humans have been the center of my life ever since I grew up with Ruby and Father, and bonding with them makes me whole. But Cho isn't into bonding. Sometimes I wonder what she's into.

Cho doesn't love being here, but then nobody does. She doesn't like Ash, Rambo's handler, who's a sweetheart and the only other female in camp. She doesn't like Brown, Lovely's handler, who's a good man. And she surely doesn't like me.

Still, that's not important right now. What's important is to let our men know that something terrible is going on up here. They should stay away.

I stare at Cho again, but she's not paying attention. No matter how I try, I can't get through to her.

Oh, well. One's got to do what one's got to do.

I raise my muzzle to the sky to sing the song of my elders, and I howl like I haven't howled since the morning I found Ruby.

My song carries over the mountains, bouncing from peak to peak, and builds into a chorus that shakes the mountains as if there were a dozen howling Prozaks, not just me.

A few heartbeats later, another howl answers.

Is it the echo?

No. It's Rambo. He's telling me he heard me, and he'll take care of things. Thank Dog.

He'll keep them safe — Ash, Brown, Emil, and Pimply Dan. Even the lieutenant.

I sigh with relief and turn to Cho. She has finally climbed all the way, but she's still not looking at me. She searches a crack inside the giant boulder and pulls out a blue package. That's where that smell came from!

She crushes it against the boulder. The stench spreads to high heaven, making me sneeze. Then, for the first time ever, she reaches to touch me without needing to. She grabs my collar and covers my muzzle with that foul-smelling rag.

I pull away, but she holds me tight. My eyes water and the fumes get me woozy. My chest burns, my stomach flips, and my brain fogs.

This is poison! I struggle to escape, but it's too late.

The world turns gray, then goes black.

4

______

I open my eyes to darkness. I don't know where I am, how long it's been, or how I got here. All I know is that I feel like a truck ran me over. Everything hurts — my hip, my back, my paws, even my tail. That's not news, considering my age and line of employment, but today it's even worse than usual.

My stomach twists. I look around for a place to upchuck, but my eyes burn and tear. I see like I'm swimming underwater.

But other than the wire grates of my cage, there isn't much to see. The place is dark, other than a flickering oil lamp gilding the wet rock walls. Water drips from the low, smoky ceiling onto the gravel-covered ground. Somewhere, far away, there's light and wind, and I know that's got to be the mouth of the cave.

Oh well. Fortunately, seeing has never been my go-to. I close my eyes and sniff the air since that's how we, dogs, make sense of things. I smell the burning oil in the lamp, the moldy scent of moss, and a hint of bat guano — boy, how I hate those flying rats. But covering them all is the smell of gunpowder and weapons. And that of hate. Unlike Americans, most Afghans don't smell like shampoo and bubblegum.

I sigh and spin, looking for a spot to lie down, when the wind brings a whiff of Cho, which stirs my memory.

What the heck happened?

I climbed the goat path, then I caught a heinous whiff. I stopped to tell Cho, but she wouldn't listen, so I howled to warn Rambo.

Then Cho put something stinky on my nose, and that was that. I went to sleep and woke up here.

What the heck happened?

I'm still struggling to understand when a bony old man with a white turban and a scraggly gray beard covering his chest shuffles my way. He stops by my cage to stare at me and scratches his head.

He glares at me. I stare back.

He doesn't blink. Neither do I.

His mouth zips into disapproval, and his bushy eyebrows join in a frown. He stinks like anger and hate, and I'd love to get lost, but I can't since I'm locked in this cage.

I wag my tail and bark.

"Come on, human. Take it easy, will you? I don't like being here either. Why don't you open that door, and I'll be on my way."

His face darkens. He may not speak Dog, but he knows I'm not afraid of him and he doesn't like it.

"Abdul?"

"Yes, Mohammed?"

"Why don't you tell me again how this filthy animal will help us fulfill our oath to Allah?"

Abdul rushes over. He's young, tall, and wide-shouldered. His dark kohl-contoured eyes dart from me to Mohammed, and he rubs his hands.

"The unfaithful Americans taught their filthy dogs to sniff for explosives, weapons, and chemicals so they could find our hideouts and raid our caches. But the dogs are just dogs. They're animals, and they only care about who feeds them. So, they can work for us just like they can work for them. They can help us find the Americans' traps, patrols, and mines. We can use their own dogs to beat them at their game, you see? This worthless animal can find the infidels' weapons, explosives, and mines. We just need to play it right. They spent years training this animal to do their bidding. All we need to do is turn him to fulfill our needs."

"And how will you do it?"

"My worthless fourth wife Aziza, the one they call Cho, will do it. The dog is trained to obey her, and she obeys me. She will make sure this filthy animal serves us and Allah, the one who should always be praised. Afterward, when we have no more use for him, we'll kill it, of course. But we'll have won the war by then, thanks to Allah the Merciful."

Mohammed shakes his head and spits to the side. I bare my teeth.

"I hope you're right, Abdul. But I don't know. This dog doesn't seem to know his place. You'd better get your worthless wife to teach it to him. Soon."

5

―――――

I lay my nose on my paws and watch them leave, wondering what happened to my pack. Throughout it all, I've been out, but now I smell the acrid fume of ammunition, blood, and death, and I know that something terrible happened, and I wasn't there to help. I didn't have a choice, but I still feel so guilty that my tail hides between my legs, and my ears hang low. There was nothing I could do when those poisonous fumes Cho forced into me robbed me of my mind, but now I'm worried sick. Who died? And who was wounded?

I just hope it wasn't Rambo.

I lie in the crate feeling guilty and sick with worry, watching the monstrous shadows the oil lamp projects against the walls. They belong to the men drinking mint tea. I know it by the smell. I wouldn't mind a drink either, but no one offered, and my throat got so dry that my tongue sticks to the roof of my mouth. I try to lick the wet cave floor through the grate, but my tongue isn't long enough, so I sigh and lay my nose on my paws. I'm about to fall asleep again when I hear Cho's steps.

"How's it going, Prozak?"

I open my eyes to a dark, shapeless blob. I sniff. It is Cho, even though she has ditched her uniform and wrapped herself in black veils from her head to her toes. I can't even see her eyes since she's covered her face. But she never looked at me anyway.

I wag my tail.

"Fine, thanks. You?"

"Never better," she says.

She brings me water and rice. I sniff them carefully. They smell OK, but I'm afraid to touch them. I don't trust her. Not anymore.

Cho sits by my crate and starts talking, but it's all too weird. I can't get over this cave, the men, and this new Cho.

"We're in a good place, Prozak. You and me, we'll make a difference. We'll fight the fight of the righteous, and we'll help them bring Allah, the Most Gracious and Most Merciful, the victory He deserves. Oh, Prozak, I'm so glad that we made it. I wasn't sure I could pull this off, but Abdul was right. If you have faith, Allah, the Cherisher, and the Sustainer of the world will find a way. He made this all happen. He saw that we got in the lead for that mission, He guided our steps, and we pulled through. Now we're here for Allah's greater glory, and we'll do our share in the Holy War. Isn't this wonderful?"

I don't know what she says, but I can smell that she's happy, and I hear the joy in her voice. Hard to believe, but it has to be true since my nose never lies.

Cho is glad to be here, in this cave, with these people we came to fight. The air's still thick with the fumes of the fight and the smell of our people's blood. But she's happy.

Really?

"What happened to Rambo? And the soldiers?" I growl.

Cho shrugs.

"I didn't watch the fight, so I don't know what happened to the others. But that doesn't matter. The only thing that matters is that we made it. We are here to fight the good fight for Allah's greater glory. Whatever happened to them, they deserved it. They shouldn't have come to this country to fight against Allah's chosen."

I tilt my head to understand. I struggle to see her eyes under the veils covering her face that muffle her words. But I can't, so I fall back on the smell.

Cho has always smelled shifty, like a dog that hid someone else's bone. Now, for the first time ever, she smells open and happy. I'm befuddled. How can she be happy here? I don't get it.

Still, Cho is my human. She's my partner. We've worked together for months. What's wrong with her? Maybe she doesn't understand what happened.

I wag my tail and try to explain.

"Cho, remember our people? Remember Rambo, the nicest Dutch shepherd I've ever met? And Ash, his handler? She was always nice to you. Remember last week when she got that splinter out of your hand? Remember Brown, Pimply Dan, and the others? What happened to them?

Cho shrugs.

"Sorry, Prozak. It is what it is. We are here for a reason, and we have a mission. I no longer am Cho; I am Aziza, Abdul's wife, and a good, faithful Muslim woman who will sacrifice for Allah's glory. Those Americans came here to destroy the Taliban and deserve no pity. We'll hunt and destroy them like rabid dogs. You're just a dog, and you don't get it, but Allah is more important than any of us. I spent years undercover to get here. My time has finally come. We'll fight for Him, and we'll defeat the infidels and crush them. You and I came here to fight the good fight, and that's what we'll do."

Cho leaves, and I watch her long black veils trail behind on the ground, wondering who she really is. I don't know this woman. And still, as I lie in my locked crate, in this cave that smells like smoke, goats, and the blood of my partners, she is my only tie to the past.

6

That made me wonder if a dog can ever really know his humans. I don't think they're as great as we see them.

I didn't choose Cho, but I did my best. When the army assigned her to be my partner, I tried to bond with her like I had with Ruby, Father, and all my humans before her, but she wanted none of it. It's like she was frozen.

She fed me and gave me water. She wasn't mean to me. But she never petted me or played with me. Seeing me never gave her joy. But then nothing did. Cho never smelled happy before today.

Now she does. Under the black veils that cover her from head to toe, she smells happy and content. She finally smells at peace.

And, like never before, she sits to watch me eat and talks to me. I don't know what she says, but I can tell she's happy.

"Come on, Prozak. You must eat to be strong enough to start training. God willing, we'll get to work soon, and we'll help our holy warriors uphold the glory of Allah."

She glances at the shadows at the cave's opening and lowers her voice.

"Abdul said we'll be starting soon. He's always right, you know. I didn't believe him at first when he said they'd send me to Kandahar and I'd get to make a difference. What are the chances, I thought, that out of all the possible places, they'd send me here? And that I'd find a way to trap the enemy and escape, with a bomb-sniffing dog, no less? But Abdul was right. Allah is All-Knowing and Most Forbearing. To him, everything is possible. So here we are, ready to serve."

She talked fast, though always softly, like she didn't want the others to hear.

Abdul came by one day. His mouth tightened when he saw Cho sitting near me, but his voice stayed soft.

"How's the dog doing?"

"He's doing fine."

"Good. You'd better look after it like your life depended on it because it does. Yours, and many others. Are you sure he'll sniff bombs for us?"

"I hope so."

"Hope isn't good enough. You'd better pray!"

Then one day, Cho clipped on my leash and took me out.

I'd been locked in that cave for so long that the brightness outside blinded me. I closed my eyes and opened my nose to the scents of the mountain. After the musty cave, the air smelled clean and green, like pines and rain. A gust of cold wind ruffled my ears. Somewhere up above, a bird called, and his mate answered.

I opened my eyes.

We stood in a high green meadow. Sharp mountain peaks surrounded us on three sides, reaching for the sky like hungry claws. The valley, far below, was white with fog. The air was cold and thin, and twisted dwarf spruce shivered their needle-like leaves under the toothy sun.

I'd never been here, but I knew we were up in the mountains, not far from where they took us. I sniffed for Rambo and the others, but I got nothing. Their smell was long gone.

"Prozak, Seek!"

I cocked my head.

"What?"

Cho pointed to the rocky trail.

"Prozak! Go seek!"

I knew "Seek." That was the search command. But what did that have to do with anything? We weren't on patrol in the desert. We weren't even inside the wire, where the handlers trained us, hiding spent cartridges and fake IEDs to keep us sharp. We were in the middle of nowhere, living in a cave inside this Dog-forsaken mountain. What on earth would I be looking for?

And Cho looked all wrong without her uniform and wrapped from head to toe in those fluttering black veils. I couldn't see her face and eyes. I could barely hear her, and that was a problem.

Dogs don't speak English. Nor Afghan or any other human language. We speak Dog.

Dog language isn't about words. It's all about smells, tone, and expression. Ears help, and so does the tail, but most humans lack in that department. And with those veils, I couldn't see Cho's ears and tail if she had them. I could barely tell if she cocked her head to ask a question.

Plus, dressed like that, she didn't look like a soldier. She looked just like the Afghan women I had learned not to trust.

That made no sense. So I sat and stared at her.

"Prozak, seek," she said.

I cocked my head to understand. Abdul came out of the cave.

"What's he doing?" he asked.

"Nothing."

"Why?"

"I don't know."

"Get him to do something!"

"Go, Prozak! Seek! Seek."

I lay down.

"What's wrong with him?" Abdul asked.

"I don't know. He's never done this before. Maybe he's sick? Or he forgot how to do it? Or maybe he's not in the mood?"

Abdul mumbled something under his breath and kicked the gravel.

"If you know what's good for you, woman, better make sure he doesn't do this again. We don't have time for a filthy dog's foul moods. Or a stupid woman's."

7

____

Cho froze. She turned her head from me to Abdul, rubbing her hands like she wanted to break them.

"But..."

Abdul spat to the side and returned to the cave without looking back. He didn't say another word, but his stiff shoulders and fire-red ears said it all, even if you couldn't smell his rage. He was so angry he could burst, but there was more.

He was scared.

Cho watched him leave, then turned to me.

"Why did you do that?"

I cocked my head in disbelief.

"Me? I did what?"

I don't know where I am, why I'm here, or who these humans are — other than they're the enemies we used to chase not long ago.

I don't even know who this new Cho is. She smells like mint and mutton instead of shampoo and deodorant; I can't see her face, and I can barely hear her from behind her veils. And I should follow her orders?

My memory is not what it used to be, but I haven't forgotten how she poisoned me and put me to sleep, so I failed to help my partners. I don't understand half of what's happening, but I know I can't trust Cho or her people.

But she's mad.

"You're supposed to work like you did in camp. Your job is to sniff and find explosives. That's what we're here for. It took me years of work, training, and jumping through hoops to get you here. Let alone the risks if they found out. And now you're lying down doing nothing like a slug? No wonder Abdul is mad!"

I cock my head and try to meet her eyes to understand her, but I can't. I don't do words. Not many. I know sit, stay, and walk. Also, ball, treat, and a few others, but that's not how I communicate. For that, I need smells, sight, tone, and touch. And this new Cho denies me all of these. She's wrapped in black cloth, smothered in mint tea, and she whispers like she doesn't want to be heard. And she won't touch me with a ten-foot pole unless she wants to poison me. Like really?

I lay my nose on my paws and watch her pace back and forth, gesturing and talking to herself. I'm half asleep by the time she comes to stare me down, forgetting she's veiled.

"Listen, Prozak. You need to do this. You will work with me to find those darn weapons, explosives, and whatever else. You need to, you hear me? Otherwise, you'll be in a world of hurt. And so will I.

"Abdul won't kill me. He loves me, even though I'm just his fourth wife. But I'm the only one he chose. The others were pawned off on him by his parents, elders, and others. He didn't even meet them before the marriage, and they're all ugly. So he'll take care of me no matter what.

"But you? He hates dogs. All Afghans do. You harbor the Demon's ugly seed. Your filthy drool will foul the holiest place. But Abdul saw the greatness of his plan beyond your ugliness. He talked me into looking after you and even touching you, as filthy as you are. But if you don't come through, you're toast. You're dead meat."

The sun had sunk behind the mountains when we returned to the cave. The air was thick with smoke and the aroma of grilled goat, but I got no dinner that evening. Cho locked me in my crate and left me there. The sunrise came, then the sunset, then another sunrise, and I still got no food and no water. I got weaker and weaker. I no longer felt thirsty and didn't even open my eyes when I heard Cho's steps.

"Prozak?"

The crate door screeches open. Cho, in her uniform, clips her leash to my collar.

"Let's go."

8

———

I tilt my head.

"Go where?"

Cho drags me out and walks me out into the sun.

The three days locked in my crate with no food or water did a number on me. I'm so shaky I can barely stand; my hips are stiff, and every step hurts. Still, I shuffle along, struggling to keep up with Cho. We cross the meadow and take the rocky trail up the mountain. It's steep, narrow, and shaded by scraggly evergreens.

The air is thin and cold, though the sun's halfway up. The mountain is so quiet you'd think there's nobody here but us. But my nose tells a different story.

The sharp wind from the top brings news of squirrels, vultures, and strange creatures I've never seen. My hackles go up, telling me that the mountain may be quiet, but it's alive and dangerous.

I look at the sunny valley below, and my heart skips a beat. I've never seen a place like this. Beyond the green pastures and the many tiny houses breathing blue smoke into the crystal-clear air, there's row after row of misty blue mountains. I count to five, but there are more. I sniff their way and catch a whiff of home. It's too far to be sure, but I know home is somewhere that way. Except it's not a way. There's no road, no trail, just row after row of snowy mountains, deep precipices, and the promise of home.

Could I make it through? My hips hurt, but they always get better after a walk. And if I find some food and water.... This isn't the desert. There's got to be water down in the valley. I could...

"Prozak!"

I turn to Cho.

"Seek."

Her dark eyes look straight into mine, and her finger points to the trail. There's no doubt about what she's asking. She wants me to look for explosives.

So I do.

Old habits die hard. I've been trained to obey humans since I was no bigger than a shoe. That's what we dogs do. We follow orders and obey our humans; that's what we're here for.

I start sniffing up the trail. Crawling over boulders is a struggle since my legs are stiff, and they don't want to work. Neither does my body. I've done nothing for days, but I'm too tired to stand. Funny how doing nothing gets you tired.

I stop to catch my breath and move on. A few feet farther, I sniff a spent cartridge under a scraggly pine tree and sit to point it out. Well, it's more like a drop than a sit since I'm too tired to sit straight, but I do my best to point to it.

Cho goes nuts.

She falls to her knees, cries, and hugs me.

"Thank you, Prozak. Thank you for doing that. I need you to keep doing it, you know? I'll give you water and food, and we'll go through this somehow, you know? Just hang on."

I wag my tail. What else can I do?

Cho picks up the cartridge like it's a trophy.

"How did that go?"

Abdul appeared out of nowhere. His eyes burn with worry, and his shalwar kameez flutter in the wind. He smells like hate and fear, and just seeing him raises my hackles, but Cho is delighted.

"Great. Prozak struggled up that path — I don't think cutting out his food and water did him any good — but he found that cartridge like a champ."

Abdul's shoulders soften.

"Cutting out his food and water was precisely what he needed to remind him that he must work for his food like we all do. From now on, there'll be no food or water unless he does his job. And that works for you too. I've been way too lenient with you. All the other men wonder what's wrong with me to let you have your way, again and again. Women are supposed to obey. I allowed you to wear your uniform and uncover your face — may Merciful Allah forgive me — because you said that filthy dog would work better that way. But you know that's not how we do things here. So, you'd better get this filthy dog into shape, or he's dead. And so are you."

Cho gasps.

"But I did everything you asked me to. I abandoned my partners and...."

"They weren't your partners. They were a bunch of fat American leeches sucking the life out of our people."

"But still, I abandoned them, and I drugged the dog and...."

"None of that matters unless you get the dog to work. Until you get it working, that dog's as useless as tits on a bull. And so are you."

"Me? But I'm your wife! You said that..."

"I said whatever I had to say to get you going. And you're only my fourth wife. I have three more, all better than you, all good faithful women who gave me sons. They're all I need. You're just a spoiled American brat that I need like a hole in the head. Make yourself useful if you don't want to share the dog's fate. Or worse. Those stupid Americans think you're one of them, and they'd do anything to get you back, but they won't. The Taliban will parade you as a war prisoner and punish you like Allah's enemies deserve. The last infidel we burned in his cage took sixteen minutes to die on live TV for all the world to see. You'd better get this dog working if you don't want to see how long it takes you to die."

Cho's narrow eyes shone with tears as she watched him leave. She sat on a boulder and looked over the faraway blue mountains.

I smelled her pain. I lay beside her to comfort her.

"You know, Prozak, I was only 18 when I met Abdul. I'd just started college. One night, I went out with my friends, and he joined us and bought me a drink. We got talking. I told him I wanted to travel and see the world, but I had no money. He laughed."

"Why not join the army? They'll pay for your education and your travel. You'll get to see the world for free. That's what I did."

"He was strong and handsome, with burning black eyes and a voice like silk. He treated me like I was a princess. I'd never met a man like that who was interested in me. It was like the sun came up. I fell in love.

"He taught me about Islam and Allah, and I fell in love with Allah too. My parents and I were Korean refugees, and I was confused between so many gods. There was Buddha, and Christ, and God, and so many others I lost count. But Abdul said there was no one like Allah the Kind, who is the Lord and Sustainer of the heavens and the earth. I believed him because there was no one like him. I converted to Islam.

"Then Abdul asked me to marry him. I said yes. What else could I say? I felt blessed. I was blind with love and happiness. We made plans for our future. We would have kids and travel and have a wonderful life.

"Then he told me that he was married. That was hard to take. But he explained that his parents had him married when he was just 18, and he couldn't say no.

"That was hard, especially when he told me about the kids. But I loved him. And he didn't love her; he loved me. And Muslims can have up to four wives.

"'Will you take another wife after me?' I asked, though I knew he wouldn't. I was all he ever needed.

"He laughed."

"Of course not. Muslims can't have more than four."

"Four, what?"

"Four wives. You're my last wife, for now, Allah willing."

"That should have kept me away, but I was stupid. Abdul loved me, not them, I thought. And look at me now."

Cho put her face in her hands.

"What am I going to do?"

9

I sit next to Cho, breathing in her misery. I listen to her heart and try to understand what's going on. Without her black veils, I can see her face and meet her eyes. I can even hear her better.

But I still don't understand her.

Unlike any other of my humans, Cho had never smelled secure and confident. There had always been a disconnect between her scent and her orders. That got me confused. Unlike humans, we dogs don't lie; we say what we mean, and we mean what we say. So we don't know what to do when messages disagree.

She's been like that since I met her, but it's never been this bad.

I can smell she's miserable because of Abdul, but that's as far as sniffing can take me. Maybe Abdul is a lousy partner, and she's mad that she's stuck with him? I know how it feels. I once had a terrible partner too, but then they reassigned me. I bet she'll get a better one next time. So, to comfort her, I lick her hands, and for once, she doesn't pull away.

"I feel for you, Cho. I'm sorry you got stuck with Abdul, but I bet they'll give you a better partner next time. You know how we always change partners? You'll get someone you like better; you'll see. Just hang on."

Cho wipes her eyes on her sleeve.

"Thank you, Prozak. Thanks for your kindness, though Allah knows I never expected compassion from a dog. But you're the only one who's showed me kindness since we arrived here. It hurts to say it, but this is worse than the camp. There, at least, I had Ash. She was nice. So was Brown. Even the soldiers tried to help when they saw you in trouble. But here? They all look at me like I'm dirt. Even Abdul. I left everything for him: My home, my family, my friends. Even my religion. I left them all behind to be with him. I did everything he asked me to, and now he acts like he hates me."

I don't know what she's saying. But for the first time ever, her voice, smell, and gestures all send the same signal. I finally feel I can trust her, and that feels good.

"I was only eight when my parents immigrated. They had a hard time getting used to American life. So did I. I wasn't like the other girls, you know. They were all blonde and smiley. I was this scared little girl who never smiled with a name that even the teachers couldn't pronounce. I couldn't speak English and didn't understand their jokes, so the kids looked at me like dirt. Just like these people do now. I ate noodles and kimchee while they had sandwiches wrapped in clear plastic, fruit juice, and dessert. I didn't even know what dessert was. So I sat alone. But I wanted to be just like the others! I learned English. I taught it to Mom and Dad. I tried to make them be like our neighbors.

"But they didn't want to. No matter where they lived, their hearts were still in Korea. And no matter how good my English was and how much mascara I wore, I was still short, brown, and slanty-eyed. The boys didn't care for me. They fought over the tall blonde girls with easy smiles and hair like silk. I was the only senior without a boyfriend.

"So when Abdul looked at me like I mattered, my heart melted. He told me I was pretty and asked me out, and I was hooked. The cute girls had nothing on me. I had the most handsome boyfriend.

"Mom didn't like him. When I brought him home, she got worried.

"Who is this man? Where is he coming from? And why did he choose you from all those girls?"

"That hurt. 'Because he thinks I'm pretty. He loves me and wants no other girl but me,'" I said.

"Mom shook her head. 'Listen, Cho, you're a great girl. Your father and I love you to the moon and back. You're smart, hard-working, and devoted. I couldn't hope for a better daughter. But pretty? I'm sorry to hurt your feelings, but truth matters. You're lots of good things, but you're not pretty. If this man told you you're the prettiest girl he's ever seen, he lied. You should ask yourself why.'

"My heart splintered in a thousand shards. I had never thought myself pretty, but when Abdul said I was, how could I not believe him?

"I told myself that Mom and Dad were old-fashioned, stupid, and mean. They didn't know any better. Abdul was the sun of my heart. I chose him, and I did what he wanted over my parents' objections. Everything he asked. And look at me now."

When I finally shuffled back to the cave, Cho waited patiently for me to scramble over the boulders and struggle through the narrow passages. She filled my water bowl, watched me drink, and then filled it again.

"Thanks for listening, Prozak. It's been a long time since anyone listened to me."

10

We started training again. Cho took me out every morning. I looked for explosives, ammunition, or whatever weapon she'd hidden along the rocky path up the mountain. When I found it, Cho rewarded me with strips of smoked meat and lots of praise. She even started touching me — she petted my head and rubbed my ears as she told me about this or that. I didn't understand what she said, but I knew she was lonely and wished she were anywhere else but on this Dog-forsaken mountain.

But then, one day, she was so excited, you'd think she'd managed to catch her tail, though I didn't think she had one. Her cheeks flushed, her eyes sparkled, and she had a hard time sitting still. She even smiled, which she seldom did. Cho wasn't that kind of girl.

We did our usual routine: I sniffed every rock, every crevasse, and all the bushes with Cho in tow. When I found the cartridge she'd hidden in the elbow of a twisty evergreen, she petted me, gave me my treat, and then we stopped for a break. I lay in the sun to warm my old bones, and Cho sat on a rock and started talking.

"I have great news, Prozak. I wasn't sure, so I didn't want to tell you, but the second month has come and gone, and now I know. It can't be a coincidence. Guess what?"

I cocked my head.

"What?"

"I'm pregnant!"

She stared at me expectantly, so I wagged my tail. Whatever she said, she was happy, so I was delighted.

"Good job, Cho. Good girl. Very happy for you!"

"Oh, Prozak, I've been looking forward to this for years! I wanted to have a baby in college, but Abdul said no. He said that if I got pregnant, I couldn't join the army, and they wouldn't send me to war, so it wasn't a good time. Maybe later, after we win the war, when we can live in peace and give our baby a better future. Not now.

"So I went on the pill. I took it all through college but stopped when I got deployed. I knew I wasn't going to get pregnant in camp! But then we came here, and one thing led to another. Abdul was so happy when I brought you that he forgot to ask about the pill. So now I'm expecting. What do you think?"

I had no idea what she said, but I was good with it as long as she was happy. So I wagged my tail and licked her hands.

"Good job, Cho."

She hugged me.

"Isn't it wonderful? I'm so happy I could scream! I didn't even tell Abdul yet, because I wanted to be sure first. I can't wait to tell him, though. He'll be so happy — how can he not be? This will be our first baby! Sure, he has kids with his other wives, but they don't count. This is our first baby, and I know he'll be wonderful."

She cupped her hands on her belly like she tried to shield it, and her face darkened.

"But I'm afraid of the war. The Taliban are ready for the big offensive. You and I are supposed to play a significant role. Abdul has told me over and over how he's looking forward to seeing us in action, but I'm worried. I'm afraid we'll be in danger.

"Don't get me wrong — I'm proud to fight for Allah's glory. But the baby? As much as I'm willing to fight for Him, my first responsibility is my baby. I need to keep him safe. Allah has power over all things. He has the dominion of Heaven and earth and millions of believers fighting for him. My baby only has me. I must keep him safe, which means that I need to be safe. My baby won't make it if anything happens to me. He needs me now more than ever. He'll need me later too, but once he's born, someone else can hold him, nurse him, and sing to him.

Cho's eyes filled with tears.

"You know, Prozak, it hurts me to think about my baby growing up with another woman. If something happens to me, Abdul's other wives will take care of my baby as Allah commands. But that thought scorches my heart."

Her happiness vanished like it had never happened, and her bitter smell of misery filled my nose. Whatever had made her happy was gone.

I licked her hand.

"It's all right, Cho. You'll be OK. Whatever happens, I'm here for you."

She sighed.

"You're right, Prozak. Why worry about all the things that may go bad? That may never even happen. And if it does, we'll cross that bridge when we get to it. But for now, I'm the only one who can keep him alive. My blood flows through his veins, my body keeps him warm, and my heart keeps him alive. If I die, he dies. So I have to stay alive no matter what."

She wiped her eyes and straightened. She had made her decision.

"I'll have to tell Abdul. He'll understand that I can't endanger our baby. He wouldn't want me to. I'll go back to war after my son is born."

She sighed, and, for the first time ever, she hugged me close to her heart.

"Thank you, Prozak. Thank you for helping me. I'm at peace now."

Her forehead still rested on me when Abdul's voice made her jump.

"What the heck are you doing, woman? Are you really hugging that filthy animal? Have you lost your mind completely? What the heck is this about?"

Cho let go of me as if I were hot.

"I'm sorry, Abdul. I'll go and wash. I'll scrub my hands, my face, and my feet. I'll wash my clothes and pray to Allah for his forgiveness. For a moment, I forgot that dogs are filthy animals that poison everything they touch. I'm so sorry!"

She bowed deep and covered her face with her hands. Abdul wasn't appeased.

"How could you forget? I spent months and months teaching you Allah's teachings. I told you that dogs are nothing but demon spawn, and their drool fouls everything they touch. And now you're hugging him? What's wrong with you?"

"I'm sorry, Abdul. For a moment, I lost my reason, and I forgot. It won't happen again, I swear! But guess what? I have wonderful news. You'll be happy and proud."

"What is it?"

Cho smiled.

"I'm pregnant."

Abdul froze.

"You're what?"

"I'm pregnant. There's a baby growing inside me. Our baby," Cho said, cupping her hands over her belly.

Abdul's face fell. He stared at her happy smile, and his mouth zipped into a line.

"Say that again, will you?"

"We'll have a baby. You and I."

Abdul sighed.

"Are you sure?"

"Yes. For two months now, I've missed my bleeding. I'm sure. I know I'm carrying your son."

"How do you know it's not a girl?"

Cho's smile faded.

"I...I don't. But I'm sure it will be a son. I don't want no girls."

"Neither do I. And, truth be told, I don't need a son either. Not now. I already have three. What I need is a dog handler. I don't need another son, a foreign wife, or anything else that would take me away from my mission. I only need you to get this dog to do what he's here to do. You understand?"

"But our baby...."

"Get your wits together, woman. There's no baby. And there won't be one if Allah the Most Merciful knows what he's doing. And he always does. No baby. Just a woman who inserted herself in our midst, pretending she could handle a bomb dog that could find explosives and a filthy dog that did not earn his keep, just like you.

"You'd better get your wits about you and do what you're here for, or you won't live long enough to be sure you're pregnant. I put myself and the other believers in great peril to get you here, and you brought nothing but shame. It's time you paid your dues and did your job, or I'll be the one who'll fire the match to set you on fire. After we burn the dog, of course."

11

———

Cho watched Abdul leave with her arms hanging by her side like dead tree limbs. Her hollow eyes begged him to stop, but he didn't. His shoulders stiff and his fists white with anger, he stomped away without glancing back.

Cho turned to me.

"Did you hear that?"

I wagged my tail.

"Yes."

Sure, I had. I didn't understand a single word, but I could see that Abdul was stark mad and Cho heartbroken. Whatever he said had wiped away the joy in her face and turned off the light in her eyes. Abdul blew it away like a candle.

"My husband said he doesn't need my son. And, if Allah knows what he's doing, he'll never let my son be born."

Her voice broke. She sat on the tree trunk and covered her tears with her hands, but the smell of her pain came out loud and clear. I licked her hands, and that made her cry even harder. So I leaned against her and lay my head in her lap.

"I'm here for you, Cho."

She cried and cried.

By the time she wiped her face with her sleeve and stood up, the shadows had grown long, and the air had a bite.

Cho shivered. She hugged herself, resting her swollen eyes on the sunset-gilded valley, then glanced at the sharp peaks behind us and sighed.

"It's a long way out of here, Prozak. And I'm not even sure which way it is.

"You know, Prozak, I wanted to believe that my mom was wrong, my friends were jealous, and everyone but me was mistaken. I knew Abdul was the man for me, but I always held a seed of doubt. How can they all be wrong, and I'm right? But I hugged him tighter and pushed those ugly thoughts away from my mind. The whole world didn't know him like I did. They were just jealous of his beauty, his spirit, and his bravery. I didn't need to listen to them.

"But I couldn't help having doubts, even though I knew that was against the prophet's teachings. You must always trust Allah's mercy and do the right thing by him, even if it's hard. So I did. But somewhere inside, I still wondered what I'd do if something went wrong. How would I escape to get back? I looked it up.

"It's not easy. It's hundreds of miles through these harsh mountains to the Paki border. And that's not much better than Afghanistan, but at least we'd be away from the Taliban. If we walk ten miles a day through these mountains, it will take us at least two weeks to cross the border. That's scary. You're old, and I'm pregnant. I can't see how we can pull this off.

"The other choice is to head back to the base. We'd just tell them that we got captured and escaped. They'd welcome us as heroes. The base is closer, but it's risky. We'd have to walk out in the open where the Taliban could easily spot us. But on the other hand, some American patrol may find us first. How would you like a ride back?"

Cho pointed to a mountain far away.

"See that curved, brown peak out East? The one that looks like an owl? That's the direction we need to go. You think we can do it?"

I wagged my tail. All I heard was "go" — the rest was "Blah, Blah, Blah," but I knew it was important to her.

"Sure thing, Cho. Whatever you say."

She smiled.

"So you're ready to do it?"

I cocked my head.

"Do what?"

"Escape. Go back to our people. Find Rambo and Ash. Wanna go?"

Now you're talking, sister! I may not know many words, but I got the good ones. Like "Rambo," "Ash," "home," and "go."

"Let's go!" I barked.

Cho put her hands around my muzzle.

"Shhh! Nobody can know about it; otherwise, we're toast. We need a couple of days to get ready. We'll go at night, so they won't see us. I'll feed you extra to build you up for the trip, but I need you to work with me. Act like we're working for them, OK?"

"Anything for you, Cho."

I wagged my tail like I understood, though all I got was that we were going home to Rambo.

But that was enough.

12

———

The following days flew like a dream.

We left the cave at dawn every day to head up the mountain. The twisted junipers hugging the rock were white with frost, and our breaths misted the air, but climbing the rocky slope kept us warm. Cho watched as I sniffed the gravel and scoured the brush for the spent cartridges or the TNT she'd hidden. She gave me treats and praised me, then hid them again, farther up the path. Each day we went a little farther up to learn the trail, find hiding places, and plant food and water along the route to prepare for our great escape.

At night, she fed me their leftovers — strange, delicious things I'd never had before: Kabuli Pulao, rice cooked with mutton and carrots, roasted nuts, and crunchy almonds; Mantu, dumplings filled with spicy meat in spiced yogurt; Borani Banjan, fried eggplant with tomato, garlic, and mint; and Bolani, fried flat bread stuffed with spinach and lentils with a minty sauce.

Between food, exercise, and the hope we'd soon go home, my muscles strengthened and my hips loosened. The trip across the mountains didn't look easy, but it no longer seemed impossible.

Cho also changed. The old Cho was frozen and remote; the new

Cho was feverish and impatient. She couldn't stay still, and her voice got so shrill with excitement I could hear her from the bottom of the cave. I was afraid Abdul would notice something, but he didn't.

He came to watch us train every once in a while. His wooden face softened when he saw us work. He didn't touch me, of course, but one day he asked Cho how she was.

"You're doing good work, Aziza. How are you doing?"

Cho's eyes filled with tears. She looked at him, ready to throw herself in his arms.

"I'm good, thanks. I...."

"Have you started bleeding yet?"

"Bleeding?"

"Yes. Did Allah relieve you from your burden, so you can do your duty?"

"My burden?"

"Didn't you say you were pregnant?"

"I..."

"You know, like I do, that being with child when you're heading to war is nothing but a burden. You don't need that. Surely not now."

Cho's hope melted like a candle. She bit her lip and looked down.

Abdul's big hand lifted her chin to meet her eyes.

"You understand that, don't you?"

"I do."

"Good. So, have you started bleeding yet?"

"Not yet."

"You will, Insh'Allah. Our time has come. We're leaving next week. Mohammed will take us to Sangan to join Amir's men. Then we'll head south to clear the camps and smoke out the infidels. I can't wait to see you get us in there."

Cho took in a sharp breath.

"Get you in there?"

"Yep. The camps are mined, so you and the dog must clear our way. The time has come for you to show what you're made of. I can't wait to show Mohammed that I was right and he was wrong. He didn't think we could turn one of those dogs. They're too stupid and essentially evil. Those filthy animals are the Devil's spawn, and they who won't serve Allah, he said. He wasn't sure about you either, but I told him that you're a faithful woman and an obedient wife, and you'll do whatever I ask you. And you will, won't you?"

"I will?"

"You will if you know what's good for you. This is Afghanistan. Here, we live and die by Sharia law. This isn't one of those silly American courts that send you home with a slap on the wrist no matter what you did. Here, we obey Allah's teaching: Thieves get their hands cut, adulterers get stoned to death, and traitors...."

"What happens to traitors?"

"You don't want to know. Trust me."

Abdul laughed and left. Cho waited until he was gone, then sobbed and covered her face. I lay next to her and waited. Her face was ashen when she was done crying, and her eyes dark holes.

"We need to go, Prozak. We're running out of time. I was waiting for the full moon, so we could see better, but it is what it is. We're leaving tonight."

That evening, I watched from my cage as the men sat by the fire at the mouth of the cave, eating and telling stories. It took forever until the fire died. Heartbeats later, Cho, dressed in her burqa, opened my crate and clipped her lead to my collar.

We tiptoed to the mouth of the cave and headed up the trail. We'd thought we knew it well, but the night changed everything. Things we couldn't see laughed at us from the dark. The twisted shapes of the spruce shivered with excitement, throwing dark shadows that followed us. The darkness was alive and scary.

My hackles went up. I pricked my ears and took step after careful step, climbing the rocky trail up the mountain. It was hard.

The wet stone was slippery, and the gravel rolled under my

paws. The moon went in and out of the clouds, throwing gnarled shadows entangled like fighting monsters. I felt Cho's heart drum down the leash as she scrambled up the path, muttering something under her breath about darkness, lousy boots, and awful long skirts.

"I wish I could have worn my uniform, but with it, there's no way to hide. This freaking burqa is bad enough. No matter who we meet, they'll want to know what I'm doing alone and where's the man of the house. I'll have to come up with some story, but there's no story on earth to explain an American uniform."

She got too tired to talk, so we climbed and climbed, every step slower than the last. When the sky started fading, Cho was barely crawling.

She stopped to wipe the sweat off her face, then looked back. There was nothing to see but the narrow, steep trail that made you dizzy. Cho sighed.

"Just half a mile more. I know a shepherd's cave up the trail to the left. We can stop to rest there for a bit; then we'll get going when the sun goes down. OK?"

I was OK, but she was running on fumes. But she bit her lips, dug deep, and kept going until we reached a tiny meadow.

The sky was clear, and the sun was up. With a big smile on her face, Cho unclipped my lead and shuffled to the narrow cleft in the rock. I sniffed it, and my hackles went up. I growled to warn her, but she ignored me and headed to the cave.

"Who are you? And what are you doing here?"

13

Cho freezes.

A gaunt old man in dirty shalwar kameez limps out of the dark. With his bent back and gnarled hands, he looks older than the mountains, but his weapon is ready. He glances at Cho, then tightens his grip on the gun when his eyes meet mine. He glares at me, and I know he wants to shoot me. But he doesn't. His eyes return to Cho, and he measures her like she's for sale. He studies her from the top of her burqa to the dusty American boots peaking under her long black skirts, then looks away.

"What are you doing here?"

Cho takes in a raspy breath. Her shoulders tighten, and her gaze glues to the ground.

"I'm sorry, uncle, I'm afraid I got lost. I came to look for my husband. He's somewhere here with the sheep. His father got sick, and we need him back home."

The old man nods.

"I see. What's your husband's name?"

Cho hesitates.

"Mohammed."

"Is he the one-eyed Mohammed who fought the Russians or the short one who limps?"

"He limps. He limps, especially when he's tired."

"That one? Really? I thought his father was dead already. Someone said the Americans killed him last year when he tried to blow up a checkpoint, but what do you know? I must have been wrong. Why don't you wait here while I go get him? There's food and water in the cave. Help yourself."

He makes a move like he's leaving, then turns around.

"But what's with the dog?"

"The dog?"

Cho stares like she'd never seen me. I look away, doing my best impersonation of a stalker.

"Yes. The dog. That filthy orange thing there."

"I never saw him before," Cho mumbles, looking anywhere but at me. That's my cue to get lost, so I turn tail and disappear into the bushes, but I don't go far in case Cho needs help.

"He's gone," the man says, his voice heavy with disappointment. "He must have followed you, thinking you're an easy target."

Cho nods.

I watch them from a rocky outcrop above the meadow, lying in a dip between the rocks. They can't see me, which means they can't find me. Humans couldn't find me here without a dog, no matter how hard they tried, since they can't smell squat. Not people or explosives, or even their own smelly socks. Nothing beyond frying bacon and beer, so I'm safe. I can use some rest after scrambling up that trail the whole night, so I lie in the shade, hoping he leaves soon.

"I'll go then. Go inside and get some rest. I'll be back with your husband by sunset," the old man says, looking anywhere but at Cho.

"Thank you for helping me, uncle. And thank Allah, the Merciful, that I found you," Cho says.

The old man glances at her once more, then tightens his grip on the weapon as he screens the mountains, and I know he's looking for me. He doesn't trust Cho, and I don't trust him.

"Allah the Great will give us just what we deserve," he mumbles, heading to the trail. His steps are slow and jerky, but his sunken eyes search every stone, crevice, and shadow. He stops again.

"Mohammed, you said his name was?"

Cho nods without a word. He shakes his head and gets on his way.

I wait for him to be gone, then run to her. She's dropped the veil off her face, so I can see she's gray with fatigue, but she smiles, proud of herself.

"I tricked him pretty good, didn't I? He'll spend the day looking for Mohammed and talking him into coming over, but by sunset, we'll be long gone."

I cock my head.

"How did you know there was a Mohammed on the mountain?"

"I didn't. But every second man here is called Mohammed, so I knew I couldn't go far wrong. Smart, eh? That got him out of our hair and left us a good resting place."

I shake my head. I wish I didn't have to break it to her, but he lied. She thinks she tricked him, but I know he fooled her. That's too bad. Just by looking at his shifty eyes and tight fists, she should know better than to trust him, but she didn't. That's humans for you. They lie to each other and fall for the others' lies. I'm so glad I'm a dog!

Still, Cho is mine to look after, so I wag my tail and grab her skirt to pull her to the trail.

"I'm sorry, Cho, but he didn't believe you. We'd better get on our way as fast as we can. They'll be coming for us."

Cho stares at me like I've got three ears.

"Come on, Prozak! Chill out a little, will you? We're safe here until tonight, and I need to rest. You do too. Let's nap for a few hours, get some food and water, and be in better shape for the trip.

Oh, boy. She wouldn't listen, even though I know that man lied to her and he'll come back with an army.

"This isn't a good place, Cho. They know where we are, and they'll come; I can smell it. How about we climb for a couple of hours, then take a break? They'll never find us in the forest without dogs."

Cho shakes her head.

"Easy for you to say, Prozak, but I need to rest, and I need to rest now. We'll go later."

"But..."

"No 'but.' Do you have any idea how I feel? When was the last time you were pregnant?"

So there. Just like that, if I'm not pregnant, my instincts are useless and my logic worthless. Oh, well.

I follow her to the cave, sniffing it high and low, but I get nothing but the smells of the shepherds, some flatbread, and some cheese.

I lap some water, but my throat is too tight for anything else.

I stop at the mouth of the cave and look back one more time.

"Are you sure we..."

"NO! I said no."

Cho wraps herself in some stinky rugs and curls down to nap.

I sigh and step out, looking for a good watch spot that lets me see the trail and the cave.

"I'll wake you up soon," I bark.

"Don't even! I need all the rest I can get."

14

I curled between the rocks and closed my eyes, but I kept my ears pricked and my nose wide open, waiting for Cho to wake up. I glanced at the shadows every once in a while. They grew shorter and shorter. We were running out of time.

I waited and waited. When my stomach tightened and my skin got prickly all over, I knew that trouble was coming. Time to wake Cho.

Cho had curled under a pile of rugs smelling like sheep, smoke, and the sweaty humans who'd slept there. She must have had a good dream because the frown on her forehead had softened, and her mouth loosened into a smile. She looked so peaceful I didn't want to wake her up, but I had no choice. We either left or got caught.

I pulled away the rugs. Cho pulled them back. I pulled harder.

She opened her eyes, and her smile vanished like water in the desert. She sighed and sat up.

"I told you not to wake me up."

I flattened my ears and tucked my tail between my legs to apologize.

"I'm sorry, Cho, but I had to. If we don't get moving, we'll be returning to your cave."

She scrambled to her feet and shuffled to the cave's opening. Her legs weren't working any better than mine. Last night's climb had done a job on us both.

I headed to the trail. Cho shook her head.

"You've got to be kidding me."

"Not at all. You wanted to go back to our base. Well, that's the way."

She sighed and started climbing.

I went ahead to check the path. I sniffed every rock and smelled every bush, glancing back every once in a while to check on Cho.

With my hurting paws and achy back, I was slower than one of those sausage dogs that you can't even tell if they're coming or going, but Cho was even slower. Her sweaty face scrunched in pain, she stumbled and smelled hopeless.

By the time the sun got halfway down the sky, we both shook with exhaustion. Our throats were parched, and our water was gone.

We stopped to rest between two steep climbs. The air was thin in the little green meadow, and the wind had a bite. That felt good as we climbed, but when we stopped, the cold seeped into our bones, making us clumsy.

Cho dropped to the grass and hugged her knees to stretch her back. I went to check on things. I sniffed every stone and every tree, but I found nothing but grass, amber rocks, and wind-blown trees. That wind thought himself on a mission. But still...

Something was off.

I sniffed, looked, and listened but couldn't put my paw on it. Until I did.

The birds had stopped singing.

The forest went eerily quiet. Everyone had gone silent: the chirping finches, the thrilling nightingales, the golden eagles calling each other — all gone. There was nothing left but the wrath of the wind whipping the trees.

I turned to Cho.

"I don't like the sound of this. Let's get going."

She sighed.

"What sound? What did you hear?"

"Nothing."

"Good. Then nothing's happening. Let's rest until we hear something, shall we?"

She covered her eyes with her arm, soaking in the last of the sun.

I circled her again and again, torn between letting her rest and waking her to reason. I knew this was the calm before the storm, but she didn't want to listen.

I barked.

"Come on, Cho. We can't wait anymore. We just can't. We need to go."

"You go, then. Go ahead and find the way. I'll catch up with you when I'm ready."

"What? But you can't! Cho, you said you wanted to save your baby. Abdul will be mad we ran away. You can't stay here. They'll hurt you."

"No, they won't. Abdul will protect me. But you go! He won't protect you."

"But Cho, you said...."

"I know what I said. That was then, and this is now. I'm too tired to go on. And all this can't be good for the baby. You go!"

I cocked my head to stare at her. We ran away because her husband didn't want her baby, and now she thought he'd protect her? How did that make any sense?

"Go, Prozak! I'll tell them you escaped. I ran after you, but I got too tired to go on. And without you, they won't need me for their war. I can just look after my baby like every other woman. Go!"

I glanced at the white mountain peaks. They were Dog-awful

far away. Miles and miles of treacherous trails and unknown dangers. I needed to get going.

But I couldn't leave Cho.

I sighed and lay down.

She picked a rock and threw it at me. Then another.

I was stunned.

I stared at her in disbelief. Nobody had ever thrown rocks at me, so I didn't know what to do.

A stone grazed my ear. Another caught me just below the eye, and it hurt.

I flattened my ears and tucked my tail between my legs. I couldn't believe that Cho would do this.

"Go! Get lost! I don't want them to find you here!"

It had to be a mistake.

"But Cho..."

"Go, I said."

The last rock was sharp. Its edge put a dent in my muzzle.

This was no mistake. Cho really meant it. She wanted me gone.

I glanced at her one more time, then started climbing.

15

I took one step, then another, then three more. I had many more to go, but my heart wasn't in it. My mind either. Since we'd left that cave last night, I'd been planning our escape. I looked for the best path to the base and tried to outthink the Taliban.

I knew they'd come after us. Those men had spent too much time grabbing us, then holding on to us to let us go. That wasn't going to happen, just like I wouldn't let some random dog get away with stealing my bone. Abdul and his friends had a plan for Cho and me, whether we liked it or not. Once they saw we escaped, they'd pursue us until they caught us. That, I understood.

But I did not understand Cho. Why did she hurt me?

I always did my best to help her. When we were in camp, I listened to her orders, loved her, and supported her as much as I could, even though I knew she didn't care for me.

But those days were long gone. For weeks now, we'd worked together and planned our escape. I thought we were a pack. Cho even smelled like she cared about me. Sure, there was that time when she poisoned me, but I grew to love and trust her. And now? Just because she got tired, she wanted to get rid of me? And then threw rocks to hurt me?

My muzzle hurt, but my soul hurt worse. I scrambled up the rocky trail, panting hard to get air, and listened to the wind's howl with a heavy heart. I hadn't felt so lonely since my friend Jinx got shot by his handler. But Jinx had attacked the man while I gave Cho nothing but love. So, why?

Humans rarely make sense, but at least they're consistent. Whether they get drunk or act mean, they always do it. You can count on them to repeat the same mistakes over and over, no matter how it hurts them. But Cho...

A cry, faint as a whisper, hit my ear. I stopped to listen.

Cho was in trouble. She needed me.

I flew down the path like the wind. Going down was easier, even with my stiff hips and achy back. I left the trail and ran straight down the mountain, skirting trees and flying over boulders. I raced faster and faster until I slipped over a patch of shifting gravel. I tumbled and rolled, closer and closer to the cliff's edge.

It was like time slowed down. I watched the void suck me into the valley down below. It was a long, long fall. I gripped the cliff with my claws, but my left paw slipped. I slid back, about to tumble into thin air when my right hind paw found a crack in the rock.

Inch after inch, I crawled back.

But my paws bled, and my legs hurt. My right foreclaw was broken and needed care. I wanted to lick it clean, but I had no time. Cho needed me now.

I limped to the last steep climb above the meadow. I glanced down the cliff, and I froze.

Cho was still where I'd left her, but she was not alone. She kneeled in prayer before her husband, who measured her with angry eyes. Mohammed and the old man in the cave stood behind him and watched.

"I'll ask you one more time. Where's that filthy dog?" Abdul asked.

"I don't know."

The slap rang like a shot. Cho cowered.

"Listen, woman. This is the last time. Where is he?"

"Abdul, please believe me. I don't know. He left me here."

"Where did he go?"

"Up the mountain."

"Where?"

"I don't know."

"Listen, woman, I'm not a patient man, but I've been more lenient with you than you deserve, and my patience is running thin. I want that dog back."

Cho put her hands together in prayer.

"Please, believe me...."

His punch came out of nowhere. She cried and fell back.

"Where is he?"

"I don't know!"

The kick came swift and vicious. Something cracked, and Cho screamed.

"Where is he?"

Cho wobbled to her feet.

"I..."

I could no longer watch.

"I'm coming, Cho," I barked.

Cho's eyes met mine.

"Run, Prozak! Run!"

Abdul aimed and fired. The bullet hit the rock to my right. I leaped to take cover, but the next shot found my shoulder. Searing pain coursed down to my paw, and my leg gave. I fell forward.

Abdul aimed the gun. Cho grabbed it.

"No, Abdul! Don't!"

He shook her off.

I struggled to stand. A bullet whizzed by my ear and hit the ground behind me.

I crawled to take cover.

Abdul took aim. Cho grabbed the gun.

This time he didn't shake her off. The shot rang, and she fell.

16

———————

I leaped to help her, but I fell on my face. My wounded leg was as good as dead, and the other three were too weak to hold me after all that scrambling up and down that mountain. I swallowed my pain and crawled forward to see.

Cho lay face down where she'd fallen. Abdul squeezed a boot under her and flipped her over as if she were too dirty to touch. He glanced at her and sighed.

"She's dead."

Mohammad shrugged.

"Thank Allah, the Merciful. From the very beginning, this woman was more trouble than she was worth. I told you, but you wouldn't listen. You and your grand plans to get her to steal that dog and have it work for us. See what came of it? Nothing but a waste of time and tons of trouble. Now the woman's dead, the dog — who knows — and..."

"I know I hit the dog. I saw it fall."

"So what? Maybe you did; maybe he dropped to the ground to take cover. Who knows? It doesn't matter anyhow. We can't use it without the woman. And up here, in the mountains, he's just as good as dead. He can't make it out. But that's not the point."

"What's the point, then?"

"You tried to use the infidels' weapons and their ways against them, and it didn't work. All your grand plans got us nowhere. We wasted all this time, and now we have to start over. And you know why? Because that's not Allah's way. Not Mohammed's way. Not our way.

"You're too westernized, Abdul. It's time you came back to ask for Allah's forgiveness, embraced the prophet's teachings, and behaved like a faithful man. All the time you wasted on this useless American woman, you should have been guiding your children into Allah's light. You should have been with your wives or fighting alongside your brothers. But you had to concoct this complicated scheme with that useless woman and the darn dog. And what good did it do to you, to us, or to Allah? None."

Abdul fell to his knees and covered his face with his hands.

"You're right, Mohammed. I wasted our time on this spoiled American, and it didn't pay off. I'm sorry."

"You should be. Let's go. It's getting late."

"Go where?"

"Back home. Where else? We need to rest and figure out a new plan. One that works, this time."

"But..."

"But what?"

"But the dog?"

"What about it?"

"What do we do about the dog?"

"There's nothing we can do. The dog will die on its own. That fat animal doesn't stand a chance alone in the mountains with no food, no water, and no shelter. And if you did shoot him, it won't be long. The Mountain Ghosts will take care of him. But I hope you're wrong, and he gets to suffer like he deserves. Let's go."

The old shepherd shook his head.

"I don't know, Mohammed. That dog is just as valuable as he was when we planned to use it. We shouldn't lose him. We can show the world what we do to our enemies if we catch him alive. That would put God's fear in the unfaithful hearts."

"How will you catch him?"

"I'll send word to the shepherds to be on the lookout. The dog will need water and food. He'll head to the springs, where the flocks are. And the people. They just need to know he's coming."

Abdul nodded.

"You're right. We could flay it, then roast it on live TV. Now, if we only had a prisoner to force into eating him, that would be grand."

Mohammed shook his head.

"There you are, thinking like a westerner again. Enough. Let's go."

"But..."

Mohammed frowned.

"What now?"

Abdul pointed to Cho's body.

"What do we do with her?"

"What do you want to do?"

"I...I don't know."

"Let her be. She got what she deserved. The vultures will take care of the rest unless that dog of hers gets hungry."

One after the other, they filed down the path Cho and I took just this morning, though it felt like a lifetime ago.

I struggled to my paws and limped down to Cho.

She lay on her back with her head tilted to the side. The wind blew her long, dark hair over her narrow face, and a silver moon glittered in her frozen eyes. That, and her smile, were all that remained of Cho. Even her smell had changed.

She no longer smelled sad, worried, or hopeless. She didn't smell like Cho.

Cho was gone.

I lifted my muzzle and howled at the moon to cry my sorrow. My last friend and partner was gone, and I was all alone in this strange place I didn't know. All I knew was that everything here was my enemy: the forbidding mountain, the harsh trail, the armed men full of hate, the unseen eyes watching me from the dark.

Cho's struggle was over. Mine had just begun.

17

I left Cho behind and headed back up that Dog-awful mountain. If I had thought it hard before, I knew nothing. Climbing that pitiless trail with a useless paw, a guilty conscience, and a broken heart was brutal.

I knew I'd failed Cho. She'd been mine to love and protect, but I'd left her behind, and she was killed. And I'd been wrong about her. I thought she'd stayed behind because she was tired and threw rocks to get rid of me. But she had sent me away to protect me. She thought I had a better chance without her. And she also hoped that, with me gone, Abdul would let her look after her baby.

Well, she'd been wrong on all accounts. Abdul had killed her. As for me, I was heartbroken, guilty, and forlorn without her. My only solace was knowing she didn't mean to hurt me; she'd just tried to keep me safe.

I kept going, but I didn't make much progress. Between my stiff hips and my useless paw, my walk was more like a crawl. And I knew that for a long time yet, there'd be no water, food, or shelter, and that didn't help one bit. But what else could I do?

Cho and I had escaped to return to our base and our partners. I knew that Rambo waited for me every day and every night. I could almost see his sharp ears pricked for the screeching of the gate, and his black muzzle up in the air, sniffing the desert for my scent. I could almost hear the beating of his faithful heart, no matter how far he was, and I'd do anything to be with him again.

So I kept putting one paw in front of the other, even though every step hurt and the wounded leg could bear no weight. I kept climbing and climbing, panting to make up for the thinness of the mountain air that smelled like snow and juniper and spruce.

How will I tell Rambo about Cho? I wondered. About Abdul and Mohammed? About that stinky cave?

Strangely enough, that took my mind off my pain and made me feel better. Climbing the steep, uneven path was hard, and my paws hurt, but smelling the night and listening to the silence of the mountain was better than rotting in that cage.

That's one good thing about growing old. You learn to take things as they come rather than fret about what could have been. Who knows? I might even get back. Not likely, but who knows? And if I don't, and this is my last journey, I'd better make the most of it.

A cloud covered the moon. The stars shone brighter than ever, and, as always, they reminded me of Ruby.

Ruby and I grew up together. Truth be told, she didn't grow much. Humans are slow to develop, and some never do. That's why they need us, dogs, to look after them. Looking after our humans is the work of our lives. We care for them and love them until we grow old. We cross the rainbow bridge, hoping the next dog sees them through. Or the one after that. Then we wait for them in the stars.

I was eight weeks old when Ruby and Father came to pick a dog. Mom sniffed them like she did with everyone who came to check us and glanced at me.

"The girl is strange, and the man smells sad. They have good bones, but they need lots of work. Still, they may be a good fit for the right pup," she growled.

I checked them out. The girl had golden skin and short purple hair. She smelled like oranges. The man was tall and stooped, with thick dark glasses and deep lines between his brows.

"How about that one, Ruby?" he asked, pointing to my brother Blue, who pushed himself forward as usual.

Ruby shrugged.

"He's cute. But how about that one, Father?"

She pointed at me.

I'd curled into a ball and squeezed into the farthest corner to watch what happened.

"Sure. But why that one?" Father asked.

"He seems lonely."

Father picked me up and handed me to Ruby. She touched her nose to mine and smiled.

"Aren't you special?" she asked.

I squeaked and tried to scramble out of her grip, but she held me tight, right over her heart. She petted me, then handed me to Father, who laid his cheek on me.

"He's so soft."

I tried to bite his nose. Ruby laughed.

"Isn't he cute?"

Father nodded.

"He sure is. What's his name?" he asked the breeder.

"That one's Orange. But they're too young to know their names. You can call him whatever you want."

"What should we call him, Ruby?"

Ruby shrugged.

"Buddy? Lucky?"

Father shook his head.

"That's too mundane, and it doesn't mean anything to him or to us. He deserves his own special name, like you and me."

"So what should we call him?"

"Let's call him Prozak. I bet he'll do more for you more than your medications."

All of a sudden, a gunshot breaks my train of thought. I stop to sniff and locate it. It's somewhere up to the left, I think, but it's hard to tell, because the echo comes at me from everywhere. The whole mountain sounds like a battlefield, so I crawl under a dwarf pine to hide and wait.

But nothing happens. When I finally dare to crawl out, the black sky has turned pink. My belly growls, reminding me that I spent another whole night scrambling up this mountain without water or food. It's getting old.

18

I sniff right and left, wondering what that gunshot was. I even look and listen, but there's nothing but the sun coming up, like it does every morning, and a frozen wind working overtime. Whatever those shots were, they weren't after me. But they were close.

I wish I could wait longer, but I can't. I need to go. My wounded leg feels dead; the others will too unless I get moving. I need to find food and water, or I'll lose whatever little strength I've got left. I may die if I move, but I'll surely die if I don't.

I scramble back to the path. That shot was close, and whoever those armed humans were, they were not my friends. No matter what they're after, they'll shoot me if they see me.

I put one paw in front of the other, limping up that dratted path. My nose, eyes, and ears are working overtime to look for danger, but I get nothing but the smell of the pines, the wind's howl, and the sun's glimmer on the wet rock...

Wait. What? Wet rock?

I crawl to the edge. The cliff to my right is vertical and goes forever, but it's cracked. Right above my head, there's a cleft big enough for a twisted dwarf pine to take root. The amber rock above glows in the sun, dripping water into the abyss below. It's not a river, not even a stream; it's just a trickle the tree can't wait to slurp. But it's my turn.

I crawl over the pine to lick the rock dry, over and over, until my parched tongue gets back in business and my stomach feels full. It's nothing but water, of course, but it's cold, clean water from the snowmelt above, and it's the best I can remember. Thank Dog, I sigh with relief. Now, if I only found some food...

Like He's heard me, I sniff blood somewhere up to my right, and I freeze. Blood, to me, is not food. Kibble is. Blood is danger.

But there's no way I'll find kibble up here. I may as well hope for a pizza parlor or the ice-cream truck. Not happening.

So I slither toward the scent like a snake. It's a brutal climb, but at least it's in the right direction. Step by step, the scent gets riper, until it gets so potent it makes me dizzy. That's when I find the carcass.

Oh boy. It smells like it's been sitting here for a while. It looks like that too.

The ginormous spiral horns and whatever's left of its shaggy coat tell me that this used to be one of the mountain goats that take these mountains for their playground. The darn things skip from cliff to cliff like they're playing hopscotch. I can't imagine how they do it.

Except this one didn't.

Odds are he missed his footing and crashed down the rocks, breaking his neck in the fall. But the odds are mistaken.

That shredded throat and the open empty belly tell a different story. Someone killed this goat. Someone as agile as him, with fearsome teeth and a taste for innards. I don't know who that is, and I hope to never find out. If I was smart, I'd run as fast as I could.

But I'm too tired to run. And I'm hungry.

I sniff and listen. I hear nothing but the wind in the branches, the water dripping from the cliff, and the silence. Nothing that says "run." Nothing but common sense, and I'm too hungry for that.

The aroma of rotting meat drives me crazy and makes me

slobber so hard that my tongue hurts. I lose all restraint and tear at the flesh like a wild animal. I've never had raw meat before, and I'm in awe. Why did no one tell me what meat tastes like? I wasted my life with kibble and milk bones when I could have hunted for meat. Or at least I could have stolen it. Humans have a lot to answer for, I think, as I shred the dead goat like a hyena.

I gorge myself until I'm sated, then go drink water until I'm so full I could burst. Time to find shelter. What I need now is rest.

I sniff around until I find a tiny crevasse in the rock behind a spiky fir. It's too tiny to let me stretch, but it keeps out the wind and covers my back.

I dig a nest in the bed of pine needles and spin around three times to find north. I curl up with my nose to the opening to sniff danger, and I let myself fall asleep.

19

By the time I wake up the shadows are long, and the pines and the rock have that dusk golden glow. I slept the whole day, and I feel better. Even my dead leg feels almost alive.

But I'm hungry and thirsty.

I remember the goat, and I start slobbering. My stomach growls, urging me on, but I'm weary. Whoever killed that goat will come back to it sooner or later, and I don't want to be there for that. Better hungry than dead.

I crawl out of my shelter to stretch. Upward dog, downward dog, a good shake, and I'm as good as new. Well, not quite, but I'm as good as I'm going to get. Time to get going. But where?

I sniff up, down, and sideways, but I get a bug that gets me sneezing. I need to find food, but even more, I need to not find any unfriendly humans — and they're all unfriendly up here — or fall upon any dangers I can't even fathom, like whoever killed that goat.

I pee at the mouth of the cave, so I know I can find it again, then I sneak to the cliff's edge to fill my belly with water. It takes me a while since this is the worst designed water dispenser ever. It's even worse than the long-necked bottles they attach to our transport crates, making you suck the water through a straw. Phew!

That was good. I lick my chops and look around. The setting sun peeks in and out of the clouds, throwing gnarled shadows that seem to chase me, but they smell like nothing. Unless they have ghosts up here, they're nothing to worry about.

I need to think, so I find a spot that gives me a good view all around, lie on the grass, and start cleaning my right paw. I lick the broken claw, then chew it down to the root to stop it from snagging on everything like it did yesterday. I clean each toe and chew away the stuff gathered between them. It takes me a while, but it's all good, because that helps me think.

I don't know about you, but I can't just sit there and think without doing something. My ears get itchy, then my stomach growls, reminding me that I'm hungry, or I remember I didn't clean my privates. With all these distractions, one can't do any serious planning. That's why I like to chew on my Kong or a bone when I need to really think. But I've got neither, so cleaning my paw will have to do.

I need to decide whether to keep going across the mountains or stick around for a bit to recover. This is not a bad place: I found water and shelter. Even food — though that's a bit iffy. But I could use a couple days to rest and heal. After that, I'd move faster than yesterday's snail's pace, and I'd be in better shape to handle whatever comes my way.

I'm still thinking when the wind changes and brings a whiff of that goat. It smells even riper today, and I start slobbering.

And just like that, my decision is made.

I follow the smell. It's not far, now that I'm rested. Heartbeats later, the goat aroma fills my nose and makes my stomach growl.

I slow down to a crawl, opening my nose and ears to uncover danger, but I get nothing. Good. I swallow my drool and creep into the clearing, when an odd scent hits my nose and raises my hackles.

Really? That can't be!

I sniff again.

Sure enough. It's a cat.

What the heck is a cat doing here? I didn't even know they had cats in Afghanistan. But there's no doubt. It's a cat, a big one. Female.

Oh well. So what if they have cats? They can have mailmen for all I care. They're not my problem. Food is.

The goat is still there, but not much of it. Someone feasted here and left only skin and bone. It's got to be those ugly brown vultures cruising above yesterday. Crooked-nosed greedy flying rats! Oh well. It is what it is, and it's better than nothing.

So I set to work, ripping the last of the tendons, tearing the tough skin, and chewing on the tender ribs loaded with fatty marrow. It may not be yesterday's feast, but it's delicious and filling.

I get my fill and sigh. I did an excellent job on that carcass, even though I say so myself. I should get going.

But what about taking a bone or two? I could bury it, then dig it out later to chew on and help me focus.

I grab a leg to tear it away, but the old goat has tough tendons that won't let go. It's easier to drag the whole carcass than get the leg. I try again, but no go.

Oh well. It is what it is.

I plant my feet and start dragging the goat to my shelter when a big shiver runs down my spine. All of a sudden, it's freezing up here. It's like a blizzard, but there's no wind.

My hackles raise. I'd better let go of that goat, I think, when a blood-curdling roar freezes my heart.

20

———————

I turn around.

My Dog!

A wide-open mouth full of shark-sharp fangs stares me in the face, ready to swallow me.

The thing roars again, and the mountains go quiet but for the echo that thunders from peak to peak. The vultures' cackle, the trees' moaning, even the wind's howl vanish under the terrible menace.

My stomach flips, ready to return everything I've eaten. I jump back, shaking like a leaf.

The enormous mouth closes. The creature it belongs to wags its heavy tail and flattens its ears. Those are good signs, signs of interest, and maybe even friendship. A tail wag is a good omen in a dog.

But this is not a dog. Of that, I'm sure.

What is it?

Dog only knows. It's twice my size, the color of melting snow, and spotted. It has green eyes, small round ears, and paw-prints all over its long thick body and broad chest, even on the restless furry tail that's almost as long as she is. And it smells like a cat.

But it can't be.

I've seen cats. I've seen them in black tuxedoes, snow-white, and every color in between. I've seen them big and small, young and old. I've seen Siamese, Maine Coons, and mangy street cats looking for a handout. But I've never, ever seen anything like this.

I wish I wasn't seeing it now.

I look left and right. There's nothing but bare rock, higher than I could scale when my legs are working. Today? Out of the question. My back rests against a cliff that ends somewhere in the sky. And, before me, this terrible creature I can't even name.

I'm trapped. Time to negotiate.

"Excuse me, Ma'am."

Her green eyes blink like she has all the time in the world. And I'd be darned if she doesn't look like she's smiling.

"Yes?" she purrs.

"Are you a cat?" I blurt. That may be the stupidest thing I've ever said, but it's too late to take it back.

She sits on her butt, kneading the ground with her massive front paws as if it were dough.

"Who wants to know?"

"I'm K-9 Prozak, at your service, Ma'am."

"K-9? What's that?"

"I'm a dog, Ma'am. I work in the military."

"Work?"

She chortles like I made a joke. I try to smile, but it ain't coming. This is not a joke, but if it were, it would be on me.

"So you're a dog, eh? I heard of them, but I never had one. They don't come up here."

Never had one? My stomach knots and I need to pee.

"My mom said she tried one once, but it was nothing but skin and bone, and it tasted worse than an old ram. But truth be told, Mom was a picky eater. She loved tongue, brain, and innards but had to be starving to touch the meat. Things changed, of course, when the humans started coming up the mountains, and the game got scarce. These days, we eat whatever we can get. Speaking about that, how did you get up here?"

"I...I got kidnapped by the Taliban, and I escaped. I'm trying to get home."

"Home? How lovely. OK. That was nice, but I'm afraid it's time we got to business. It was nice chatting with you — up here, you never meet anyone but goats and sheep, and they're not into conversation. You have to chase them down the cliffs, and I swear some of them are suicidal. They'd rather die than get eaten. Anyhow, you ate my goat, and I'm hungry. So how would you like to proceed?"

"Proceed?"

"Yes. Would you like to run down the cliffs for me to chase you, or would you rather fight right here?"

"But, Ma'am, I didn't eat your goat. The birds did. Well, I ate a little. But it was mostly gone by the time I arrived."

She cocks her head like a dog, and for a scant minute, I have hope.

"Let's just say we forget I saw you drag that carcass. That matters how?"

"I...I didn't take your food," I lie. But desperate times call for desperate measures.

"So what?"

"So what?" I mumble.

"Yes. So what if you didn't eat the goat? You are food, and I am hungry. So, as I said. Would you rather run or fight? And please be aware I'm giving you a choice I never gave any of the goats. That's how much I enjoyed your company."

"But I am not food. I am a dog!"

"I never said you were nutritious. Or even tasty. But when you're hungry, food is what you get. And I got you. So what will it be?"

I've never thought of myself as food before. And that reminds me of Ruby's cat Sheeran, a tiny tabby she'd found in some ditch.

He was friendly enough unless you happened to be a mouse, a mole, or a squirrel. Then, you were doomed.

His fun was not in catching you. It was in letting you go, so he could grab you again and again. I'll never forget this one squirrel. She was almost as big as he was. He pretended to forget about her, and she tried to escape. He let her go nearly half the yard before leaping to catch her again and again. It made me sick to think of it. In the end, Ruby grabbed him and released the squirrel, but it was too late.

That's cats for you.

"So, run or fight?" she asks.

"So you are a cat?" I ask like it matters.

Her green eyes shine with glee, and she flicks her tail.

"I guess it depends what you mean by a cat. I'm a snow leopard, one of the few left. Some call us big cats; others call us the ghosts of the mountains. So, on a broad definition, I guess I'm a cat."

That explains it. No matter how big or small, a cat is a cat. Just like a dog is a dog, whether he's a Great Dane or a teacup Yorkipoo. The body may be different, but the soul is the same.

She glances at me sideways as she licks her paw, making sure it's sparkly clean, then pulls out a set of dagger-like claws and inspects them. Satisfied they're in working order, she turns to me.

"So, what do we do?"

What do we do? Darned if I know.

No way can I run up and down these cliffs like those goats, and she's even more nimble than them. But I'd rather fall and break my neck than watch this witch eat my innards. Still, a dog's got to do what a dog's got to do, even when he's just an old pacifist and a golden retriever.

"We fight, I guess."

21

Her eyes round in wonder.

"You're up for a fight? Really? Good for you!" she purrs.

I don't know about that. I've never fought cats, but I know they don't fight pretty. I've never fought anyone, in fact. Other than my littermates, but that was too long ago to count.

I glance around, looking for inspiration. Slim pickings. Nothing behind but the rock wall too steep to climb. Rock to my right, rock to my left, then the monster before me. It's not looking good. But at least my back is safe, I tell myself, trying to be positive.

To pump myself up, I struggle to channel all the anger I can muster. It isn't much since anger isn't my thing — I'm a mellow sort of guy — but if there's ever been a time to let it rip, it's now.

So I think about everything that has made me angry — Ruby's tears, Father's disappearance, Jinx getting shot, Viper being thrown out of the army. But they don't make me angry. They make me incredibly sad. Like what's the point of it all? Why even bother to fight to stay alive in this terrible world?

Then I remember Cho's sad life and her terrible death at the hand of the man she loved, and that makes me so angry I no longer care if I live or die. I want to kill.

I bare my teeth, growl, and leap at that cat like she's the one who killed Cho. I know she isn't, but the man who did is just another predator from these mountains, someone just as evil as this cat, who fooled, used, and killed Cho. My blood boils in my veins, and I'm so angry I forget I'm just a wounded, mellow golden who never fought anyone. I'm crazy with rage, and I go for her throat.

I barely graze it, and she leaps back. Her green eyes widen, her ears flatten, and she fluffs herself even bigger.

"Really? Are you nuts?" she hisses.

I don't stop to listen. I leap after her, but I stumble, so I sink my teeth in her paw like it's the goat. She spits in outrage.

"Who the heck taught you to fight like that?"

She jumps on me, looking for the throat. I feel her sharp teeth graze my skin, but thank Dog, I still have my collar. I hear her bite the metal, and my skin burns, but at least she didn't shred my throat in one bite like she did with that goat. I'd better keep my throat safe. And my belly.

She spits out a tooth, and while she stares at it in disbelief, I squeeze past her to the trail heading down. My chances are slim, but I've got to do what I can. I run like heck down the path, but just ten steps later, I feel her teeth sink into the back of my neck. I fall and roll, taking her with me. We slide to the cliff's edge and teeter above the abyss below. But she sinks her claws in the ground and pulls us back. Her teeth hurt like the dickens in the scruff of my neck, and I can't turn my head enough to bite her.

She drags me up to the trail like I'm a puppy, and I get furious.

"Stop it, you evil feline. Let me go."

She doesn't, of course. That makes me so mad I'm ready to jump into the abyss with her. I plant my feet and take a leap, bringing us near the edge. Her teeth open, and she lets me go, but I've got too much speed to stop. I try to change course and veer left, but I lose my footing and roll, ready to fall when I hit a tree root.

That slows me enough to let me claw my way back, and I scramble back to my paws to find her waiting.

"You're way more fun than I ever thought, Dog," she purrs, licking her lips. She crouches, ready to pounce, but I've had it.

I growl like a chainsaw and leap at her throat. I grab a chunk of her fur and shake her for the kill. She roars and rakes my belly with her hind paws as her teeth look for my throat.

But I've got her throat, so she can't bite me. That gets her so mad she howls, yowls, and bicycles those hind legs with the four-inch claws, thrashing my belly.

She's about to split me open, I think, when a gunshot makes the mountains tremble.

I guess they found me after all.

Another gunshot, and the world goes dark.

22

___

I open my eyes to the night. I don't know how long it's been, but the dusk is gone, and the clearing went dark. The twisted shadows of the trees wrestle with each other, and I wonder why until I lift my head and see the light.

A flashlight darts a beam of light over what used to be The Cat. She dangles upside down between two trees as a small man skins it deftly. He pulls off the spotted coat with slow, gentle moves, uncovering the naked pink body underneath.

With its exposed pink belly, what's left of the cat looks like a carcass in a butcher's shop. The only thing left unchanged is her smile. She's a monster, even naked. But I don't need to worry about her anymore.

I need to worry about him.

He's skinny and beardless like a boy, but his shalwar kameez and turban tell me he's one of them. I sniff him.

He smells like sweat, gunpowder, and sheep. Something else too, something familiar, but I can't put my paw on it. The cat scent, more potent now that she's naked, overwhelms everything.

I watch his skinny arms work, and I wonder how he lifted that giant cat up there. And, more importantly, why did he kill the cat instead of killing me? Did he get her by mistake?

Oh well. It doesn't matter. I'd better get away before he shoots me too.

I struggle to stand, but my legs won't have it. The leg Abdul shot is still numb, but now my other hind leg hurts like crazy. I try to move it, and a sharp pain shoots up to my brain. It's so bad I open my muzzle to yell, but I bite my tongue instead.

What the heck happened? Did he shoot me too? Or did I break my leg when I tried to pull the cat over the cliff?

She dragged me back and clawed my belly, and that's where the scorcher is. My whole stomach burns like I'm lying on embers, and every breath hurts. That darn cat did a job on me with those dagger-like claws.

I glance at her again, but seeing her makes me sad instead of mad. There's something pathetic in hanging upside down and getting stripped of your coat, no matter how much you deserve it. And Dog knows she did.

Anyhow. Forget the cat. I need to get away. But how?

I try to stand once more, but that's not happening. I'll have to crawl. Just thinking of it hurts, but I have no choice.

I glance at the man. He pulls the skin off Cat's hind paws like he's stripping her socks. Just seeing it makes me shiver. But he's busy, and he's got his back to me, so I start crawling inch by inch. The rough gravel burns like hot coals. I bite my tongue to keep quiet, but a branch snaps. He hears it and turns.

"You're up? Good."

I don't understand his words, but I get the tone. He's pleased that I'm alive, and that makes me shiver. I bet I won't like what comes next.

He turns back to his work.

"You've got to be that infidel dog they all talk about. The Taliban said we should catch you alive. But if we can't, we should kill you rather than let you go."

His bloody hands pull the skin down Cat's short forelegs, careful not to tear it. He's almost done with her. I must be next.

I try to stand, but I crumple to my side.

"That cat almost did you in, didn't she? I checked you out. Your hind leg is broken, and your belly is torn to shreds. But you're lucky she didn't get inside; otherwise, I'd have to put you down. There's a few bites on your neck and your hip, but they don't look too bad."

The cat's carcass sways in the air as he pulls on this side, then the other. He's done, but for the head.

He studies it, then slips the point of his flame-shaped knife between two neck bones. He pushes it in and swipes it around, and, just like that, the big round head drops to the ground leaving the naked carcass behind.

"That's that. With some luck, if Allah sends me the right buyer, this skin will keep us fed over the winter. I have you to thank for that, you know. I'd been stalking this cat for weeks, but she always vanished before I could put a bullet in her. Thanks to you, she was too busy to feel me this time."

With loving moves, he wipes the bloody knife on his sleeve, slips it in its scabbard, and slides it under his belt.

"You've got to take care of your pesh-kabz, you know, if you want it to take care of you."

He stretches the bloody skin fur down on the ground and folds it around the severed head into a square package. He ties it with string, picks up the gun and the flashlight, and looks at me.

"The way they talked about you, I thought you'd be a monster, like this thing here, not just an old shaggy dog. Now you stay put and wait. I'll take the skin home, then come back for you."

Bent under the weight, he takes slow, careful steps down the trail.

I wait until he's gone, then get moving.

Crawling has never been my thing. Even less so as I got old and my hips started hurting, but it's never been this bad.

My leg kills me, and my belly feels on fire as I inch back to my shelter. But one way or another, I've got to get away before he returns; otherwise, I'm dead meat.

Worse, in fact. If the Taliban want me alive, it's not to congratulate me. I didn't forget what they did to Cho. What they'd do to me would be worse.

So I crawl, inch by inch, to my shelter. This evening, when I came for the goat, it was just heartbeats away, but now it takes me forever.

I stop to sniff and listen every once in a while. Still, there's nothing but the fading cat smell, the junipers' scent, and the wind whipping the scraggly evergreens into submission.

I'm exhausted by the time I squeeze back into my shelter. Thirsty too, but I'm too tired to crawl the extra steps to get water. And I've seen enough of that cliff to last me a lifetime.

I curl in my nest inside the rock and lick my wounds. Boy, do they hurt: The scrapes on my paws, where I held on for dear life to the slippery rock; the broken leg; and most of all, my belly, skinned and coated in crusted blood and dirt from my throat to my you-know-what.

I clean myself the best I can, but for the wounds in my neck that I can't reach, then stick my nose under my tail to catch a nap. I'm spent. I need all the rest I can get, but napping doesn't want to happen. Whenever I close my eyes, I see that cat.

She didn't get to taste dog, after all. Not thanks to me; I'd have been dinner if that human didn't shoot her. But still, I'm alive while she hangs from those trees, waiting to feed the vultures. But for the coat, that's heading down the mountain.

I still don't know why he shot her instead of me, but I don't get to wonder for long. The wind brings a whiff of his scent, and just heartbeats later, he's here.

"There you are. I told you to stay put. It does no good to use that broken leg; it will only take longer to mend and heal wrong. Come on, let's go."

He leans over to pull me out.

I bare my teeth.

"I don't think so, buster. Get lost!"

His eyebrows go up.

"Seriously, now? After I climbed half this mountain to get you? Don't even think about it, Sediq," he says, grabbing my collar to pull me out.

I wish I could bite him, but I can't. First, I never bit anyone — other than that cat, but she deserved it. And second, he smells like a friend. That's crazy, I know — I never met a Taliban who didn't smell like hate, even the kids — but this one doesn't. He smells like smoke, mint, and the cat's blood. And something else that's unsettling but not threatening. It's like a scent I used to know, but I can't remember when.

He doesn't look threatening, either. His green eyes smile, and his small, calloused hands are gentle as he lifts me on his shoulders.

The night is dark, the path is steep, and I'm heavy. He stumbles and slides, but he manages to keep his footing as he takes me down the trail it took me forever to climb.

Darn! I wasted all that effort. Even worse, my belly hurts like crazy. My leg does too, and it feels weird to sit on someone's shoulders, but I do my best to stay put.

By the time I catch a whiff of humans, smoke, and food, the sky has faded from black into purple, and a red sun peeks from behind the jagged black peaks as we reach his cave.

He pushes aside the blanket that hangs over the opening, steps in, and sets me down on the patterned Persian covering the ground.

I sniff like one does. This place smells like him and the cat skin. Also smoke, mutton, and a woman who hasn't smiled in a while.

I look for her, but the flickering oil lamp only lights the low ceiling and a thin mattress covered with checkered pillows, leaving dark the back of the cave.

The man fills a bowl with water from a metal bucket and sets it in front of me. A woman in a faded burka emerges from the darkness, sees us, and gasps.

"What's this, Omar?"

"It's the dog. That infidel dog the Taliban can't stop talking about."

"What's he doing here?"

"He's hurt and needs a place to heal."

"You must be kidding! You're not going to keep him here, are you?"

"Only until he's good to go."

"You can't do that! That's insane! The Taliban will find out and kill us both! Go tell them you found him! Even better, take him there. I don't want this filthy animal in my house! And look at you! Not only did you touch him, but you gave him water from our bowl! Now I have to throw it away, unless I wash it with dirt and let it sit in the sun for 40 days. Take that dog away!"

"I can't, Mother. The Taliban will kill him."

"So what? What's it to you? He's nothing but a filthy animal that

Allah cursed. Look at him laying on my floor and drooling his demonic drool all over my carpet. The angels can't even come in while he's here. What if I die? The Angel of Death can't even come in to take my soul. I don't need this curse! Take him away, I said!"

"Mother, I can't. Not right now. But I'll only keep him here until he's ready to go."

Omar's mother lifts her hands to her head.

"This is crazy. First, you bring that snow leopard skin that's gonna get us both in jail if the government people find out...."

"The government is thousands of miles away, Mother. And it's about to fall. That skin will keep us fed through the winter."

"Then you bring this filthy animal into my house, and you want to keep it here? That's insane. Take him to the Taliban right now!

"I can't, Mother. But I swear I'll send him away as soon as he gets better."

"Well, if you can't, I can. I'll go tell the Taliban he's here."

"Don't."

"Sure, I will. You give me no choice."

"Please, Mother, don't. Or..."

"Or what?"

"I'll go with him, and I won't come back."

24

Omar's mom didn't turn me in, but she steered clear of me like I dodge baths. Omar made me a straw bed in the dark bottom of the cave, and she never came near.

That suited me just fine. After living with Cho's people, I'd had enough of these humans to last me a lifetime. But I had nothing better to do, so I spent my awake time watching her pray, sew, or cook on the gas ring at the mouth of the cave.

Omar was seldom at home. He left at dawn, returned at night smelling like sheep and sweat, and handed his mother his brown shoulder bag like a trophy. Her face lightened as she took out the lentils, naan, cheese, or potatoes. She even smiled once when he brought a leg of lamb.

After dinner, Omar sat on his mat to play his rubab, a thing that looked like a chunky guitar, only smaller. Omar held it lovingly and coaxed it into making strangely soothing sounds that made me think of summer rain falling on a tin roof. I didn't mind it — unless it woke me up, but he always smelled like sorrow when he played it.

I cocked my head.

"Why bother to play if that makes you sad, Omar?" I asked.

He put away the rubab but didn't answer. He was a strange kid, Omar. He seldom spoke and never smiled, and his vexing smell kept me wondering. But he stayed true to his word and did his best to help me heal.

That first night, he cleaned my wounds with a rag soaked in green tea smelling like forest herbs and dressed them with honey.

His mother shook her head.

"Are you crazy? You're wasting the little honey we have on that dog?"

Omar shrugged.

"I've got nothing better. And you want the dog gone. So, I'm trying to heal him so he can go."

He pulled on my broken leg until I thought it would come off. It hurt so bad that I growled and bared my teeth, ready to bite him. But the broken bone clicked into place, and the sharp pain dulled to an ache. He splinted it, then wrapped it in a fresh sheepskin that tightened as it dried and held it in place. Itched like crazy, so I tried to take it off, but he tied an old potato bag around my neck, leaving out just my head. I couldn't chew it off no matter how I tried. And then he sat with me.

His mother didn't like it.

"There you are again, wasting your time with that filthy animal. I can't wait to see it gone."

"I know, Mother. I'm doing my best to get him better so he can go."

He turned to me.

"She wasn't always like that, you know. I remember when she was young and pretty. She even smiled sometimes, but that was long ago when Father was still with us. He was awesome, Father, and great with his rubab. He called it the lion of instruments and played it at weddings and parties — wherever people needed joy. Everyone loved his music and gave him something — sometimes money, but usually rice or honey or cheese. Sometimes even a chicken. When Father was here, we never lacked for food, and we got meat and fruit every week."

Omar watched his mother stir a bowl of lentils over the fire and sighed.

"Then the Taliban came and made music Haram — forbidden. They said music was a waste of time. People should pray to Allah instead. After that, there was no more playing the rubab, no rice, and no chickens. We went hungry. Until Father started playing for people in private. He did it for food and because he loved his music. Music was his life."

Omar's mouth curved down, and his green eyes filled with tears. He suddenly looked like a child, and I wondered how old he really was. Eleven? Twelve maybe? Too young to be the man of the house either way.

"But then someone told the Taliban, and they came after him. They gave him the lashes before the whole village until his clothes fell apart. They wanted to teach the others a lesson and ensure he'll never forget. And he never forgot.

"Then, one day, he couldn't take it anymore and went to get back his rubab. Mother tried to stop him.

"'Are you crazy? They've burned your rubab long ago. You're just going to get into trouble. Please don't go! Omar and I need you!'

"But Father didn't listen. His life was empty without music, so he had to go.

"Mother and I waited and waited, but he didn't come back. When we went to look for him, the Taliban said they never saw him. But I know they lied because that's what they do. They lie, and they kill. They're worse than sickness. At least diseases don't lie.

"That's why I'm looking after you, even though I know Mother's right. Even the Quran says that dog slobber is Najis, impure. If you touch a wet dog before prayer, you should scrub yourself seven times, not just once, to purify for prayer. I know I shouldn't help you; I shouldn't even touch you. But the Taliban's even worse. So, to avenge Father, I swore I'll make sure they won't get you. And I'll do my best."

He wiped his tears and left, a skinny kid who should have been playing with his friends and going to school, not shooting leopards and defying the Taliban. But I was lucky he found me.

25

Day after day time dragged like a snail through slime. Nights too. It felt like forever until my leg felt good enough to stand and my belly stopped hurting.

Omar was pleased.

"Looking good, Sediq. A few more days, and you'll be good to go," he said, tying the bag around my neck.

His mother frowned.

"He's been here for weeks, and he looks fine. How much longer will you keep him? You know as well as I do that we're in mortal danger every day he's here."

"Just a couple more days. That bone must get strong enough to hold him through the precipitous mountain crossing."

His mom snorted.

"Yeah, like he knows where to go. You'll let him off, and the Taliban will catch him in a day or two and wonder where he's been all this time. And if they find us...." She shook her head.

"I shouldn't have let you keep him here. Never. Now I must worry about what happens even when he's gone."

She huffed and left. Omar picked his rubab, sat on the mattress, and strummed the cords but didn't play. He talked instead.

"You know, Sediq, I can't believe I'm saying this, but I'll miss you when you're gone. I know you're just a filthy animal, but...but it's like you understand. You are the only one I can talk straight to. With you, I don't need to hide or lie; I can say whatever's in my heart, and I know you'll never judge me and never tell. I know it's stupid. You're just a dog, and you can't understand. But how you look at me, it's almost like you have a soul."

He sighed.

"I hope you make it through. These mountains are treacherous and loom with danger. That Mountain Ghost was not the only one, though they're getting fewer and fewer; thank Allah, who keeps our sheep safe. The moon bears are hungry in spring. And the humans with their traps can be worse than the Mountain Ghosts. You should never trust anyone."

I wagged my tail. He was right.

Look at Cho. She betrayed our men and trapped us to please Abdul, who treated her like dirt. Like that wasn't enough, she chose to stay behind when we escaped and ended up feeding the vultures, thanks to her husband. The man who was there to protect her killed her instead. Trusting him was her undoing, again and again.

Then Jinx, the best K-9 on the border. He, too, got killed by the man he trusted the most: his handler.

Why do all these people — dogs and humans — perish by the hand of those they cherish? Lucky me, I have nobody to love or trust, so it looks like I'll live forever.

The memory of waiting for Father's return day after day stabs my heart like a knife. It's been years, but that's still the worst time of my life, and I hope it stays that way.

Two days later, I napped in my bag. Omar was gone, as usual, and his mother sat on the mattress, mending a pile of clothes when the entry curtain got ripped off, and three bearded men stuck their heads inside.

The first one stepped in to look around.

"Where is he?" he growled.

Mother grabbed the clothes she was mending and stood to cover me.

"Where is who?"

"Your kid. Where is he?"

"Up in the mountains with the sheep. What do you need him for?"

"We've been told he's defying the law and acts like an infidel."

"That's a lie!" Mother said, throwing the pile of clothes on top of me.

"My son is a good, faithful kid. He always obeys Allah's law. Whoever told you otherwise lied."

"Oh, yeah? So how come the neighbors heard him play music last night? Where's the rubab?"

Mother froze.

"The rubab?"

"Yes. The rubab."

Bored with waiting, a second Taliban came in. He waited for his eyes to adjust, then headed toward me and kicked my bag.

"What's this?"

I bit my tongue to stop from yelling.

"Potatoes. I need to keep them cool and dark; they sprout otherwise."

The man leaned to see better.

"It's here. The rubab's here." Omar's mother handed it to them.

The second man took it, then slapped her so hard she fell on her knees.

"That's for the lie. As for the rubab, that punishment is yet to come. You'll bring your son over tomorrow morning. Otherwise, we'll be back, and you'll like it even less. You hear me?

Her eyes glued to the ground, Mother nodded. They left, and she burst into sobs.

26

———————

Omar returned after dark. He saw the torn curtain and his mother's tear-stained face and froze.

"What happened?"

"They came for the rubab."

She didn't tell him who "they" were, and he didn't ask.

"Did they find it?"

"I gave it to them."

"Why?"

"They would have found it anyhow. But if they went searching, they'd have found that demon' spawn you sheltered here. The rubab will cost us a few lashes. But if they found the dog, we'd be dead."

"Lashes?"

"Yes. Remember what they did to your father? They want us there tomorrow, both of us, to get our punishment. They'll want it public, so everyone can see what happens when you disobey the Taliban. It's terrible, but they won't kill us, I don't think."

"But Mother..."

"What?"

"I can't get the lashes."

"Then, you should have left the rubab alone, like I told you a hundred times."

"But mother..."

"What?"

"If they lash me, they'll discover I'm a Bacha Posh."

His mother clasped her mouth and froze.

"I forgot. Good Allah forgive me; I forgot. It's been so long that.... What will we do? They'll come after us if we don't go, and it will be even worse."

Omar sighed.

"You'll go. I'll leave tonight. You'll tell them I never returned from the mountains. They'll think I saw them here, and I ran away to escape my punishment."

"But where will you go?"

"Across the mountains to Auntie Farrah."

"Farrah? Only Allah knows where she is these days. Last I knew, she was across the Paki border. How on earth will you find her?"

"I'll find her. I've been thinking about going there forever; I just didn't want to leave you. But now I have no choice. I'll be of no use to you or anyone else if they kill me."

He checked his belt for his knife, then grabbed his brown shoulder bag. He dropped in his flashlight, a lighter, and some water and seized his ammunition.

His mother handed him a piece of cheese wrapped in naan, then carved a hole in her mattress with her bent kukri knife and pulled out a blue bundle.

"This is all our money and the one bracelet I haven't sold. It's good, old gold and should bring you some money. It isn't much, but it's all I've got."

Omar hugged her, his cheeks wet with tears.

"Thank you, Mom. Be safe. I'll send you word when I get there."

"Take care. I'll miss you."

Omar peeked outside.

"No one around, and the moon's in the clouds. It's time."

He came to the back of the cave, kneeled next to me, and pulled out his flame-shaped knife.

My heart froze. I tried to stand, but the bag held me down.

Mother gasped.

"What are you doing?"

"What do you think I'm doing?"

Omar put the tip of his knife to my throat.

I held my breath.

In one smooth move, he cut the string holding the bag around my neck and put away the knife.

"Let's go, Sediq."

27

We headed up the same trail he'd carried me down on. It wasn't that long ago, but it felt like forever. The sharp wind sweeping the mountain smelled like juniper and snow, and the starless night was darker than dark. There was no light other than a couple of flickering oil lamps lighting the caves down in the valley.

The mountain was silent. The forest pretended to be asleep, but I knew it wasn't. I didn't see the eyes, but I felt them following us, and I hoped they didn't belong to Cat's brothers. The wind picked up, and the trees wailed and moaned like they hurt.

I picked up the pace to catch up with Omar. He walked ahead without a word, moving like he could see in the dark. I tried to keep up, but after all those weeks in the bag, I was weak and slow, and I fell behind. Omar stopped to wait.

"I'm sorry, dog, but we need to get going. At dawn, when Mother goes for her lashing, and they find out I'm gone, they'll come looking for us. We'd better be far away."

I picked up the pace, and he slowed down to walk by my side.

"I'm sorry that I don't know your name. Do you even have a name? Do dogs have names, where you come from? Here, they don't. I've heard that they don't even name people in some places.

Women, I mean. They give them numbers and call them Second Daughter or something like that. That's got to be terrible, to not even have a name. But here, we do. Our women can't go to work or even leave their house without a man, but at least they have names.

"I did too. When I was a girl, they called me Zahab. That means gold. My parents wanted me to know I was precious.

"They wanted to have sons, but Mother bore no other children. And Father needed help with his work. He wasn't just a musician, you know. He only played the rubab when the work was done, and people got together to celebrate. Most of the time, he looked after our sheep or helped our neighbors. Father was good with his hands, so they called him whenever they had a sheep that couldn't lamb, a mule who went off his food, or even a kid who broke a bone. He gave them his special teas and ointments and made them good as new in no time. Unless they died. But they often got better. He taught me to clean wounds, fix broken bones, and soothe queasy stomachs. Anyhow, Mother and Father needed a son, but all they had was me. So they decided to make me Bacha Posh."

Someone screamed in the dark. We stopped and pricked our ears. Right behind us, someone answered.

"Just night birds," Omar said. "Anyhow, my grandmother, Father's mother, said no. 'Don't do that. You'll ruin her. She'll get used to being free like a boy. She'll go out to play and work and even go to school. And then, when she grows up, you'll wrench her from her life of freedom. You'll lock her in the kitchen and hide her under the burka to never be seen again. That's terrible. I'm almost seventy. I've seen at least a dozen Bacha Posh, and none of them was happy. Two left their families to go God knows where, dressed like men, rather than settle into a woman's life, obey their husbands, and bear children. The others stayed, and they lived a life of misery. You don't want that for Zahab.'

"Father hesitated. He shrugged and turned to Mother. Mother straightened and looked straight into Grandma's eyes.

'You may be right. Getting back to a woman's life may be hard and painful. But such is life. So is winter's cold after summer's sun, the pain of old age after youth's hope, death after life. Would you rather not live at all if you can't live forever? I want Zahab to live the life I never had. I want her to look people in the eye, feel the wind in her hair, and be free to come and go like I've never been. I know it's not forever. But nothing is.'

"Grandma sighed. Father looked at Mother like he'd never seen her.

'I never knew you felt that way, wife.'

'You never asked.'

"That night, Grandma cut my hair with big scissors that Father used to shear the sheep, and Mother cut her best burqa to make my first boy clothes. The next morning, Father took me up the mountains. He taught me to look after the sheep, hunt, and play the rubab. He taught me everything I know, and I've been a Bacha Posh ever since.

"The neighbors knew, of course, but they said nothing. Many families do that when they have no sons. Some even say that having a Bacha Posh may help the family get a son. But we didn't."

"Then Grandma died, the Taliban came, and Father disappeared. I was the only help Mother had left, and she thanked Allah she had me. If I weren't Bacha Posh so I could look after the sheep, hunt, and work for other people, we'd have starved long ago. Mother is a woman who couldn't even leave the house alone. But with me, she could, since I was a boy. Or so they thought.

"But my time was coming to an end anyhow. Mom says I'm almost thirteen. I'm growing into a woman's shape. You can't tell under my shalwar kameez, but if they lashed me until they ripped off my clothes like they always do, they'd see it. And that's a death sentence. I knew I had to leave sooner or later; I'd been thinking about that for two winters. But..."

Her voice broke. She wiped her eyes with the back of her hand, then wiped it on her pants just like Ruby used to, and I finally understood what had bothered me since the day we met.

Omar didn't smell like a boy. She smelled like Ruby. Sort of. Ruby smelled like gum, shampoo, and chocolate, while Omar smelled like sweat, sheep, and smoke. But beyond that, they were the same.

"What will happen to Mother, now that she's got no one left? Who'll look after the sheep? Who'll bring in the money? How will she even leave the house?"

Omar sobbed. I didn't know what she said, but I felt her pain.

I licked her hand.

"There, there. You'll be OK; you'll see. I'm here for you."

Omar hugged me, then cried and cried until she got me soaking wet.

Boy, did I need to shake! But I didn't. I didn't want to be rude.

28

———————

Two days later, we reached the snow, and I went crazy. I hadn't seen snow since I came to war, and I couldn't get enough of it. I ran around in circles, rolled in it, dug it, chomped on it, and had the time of my life.

Omar's eyes went round with surprise. At first, she stared at me like I'd lost it, but then she started chasing me. I turned around and chased her back, and I heard her laugh for the first time ever.

We ran and played until we got exhausted. I dropped into the snow, panting, and Omar shook her head.

"Wow. I never knew dogs could be fun."

I wagged my tail.

"You have a lot to learn, my friend."

We got back on our way. Our hearts felt lighter after all that laughter, but our journey was no laughing matter. The days were cold. The nights were even colder. The air was so thin you had to breathe twice to get in one breath's worth. We'd had no food. For days now, we ate nothing but snow. Even the pine needles were scarce up here, and Dog knows they weren't worth chewing. But they softened the burn in your belly and gave it something to toil besides itself.

Omar's gun was ready in case we found some prey, but the only things alive up here were the ugly brown vultures eyeing us from above.

"They're waiting for us to die to feed on our bodies," Omar said, her eyes stormy. "Boy, how I hate those things."

I wagged my tail and pointed my nose at them.

"Why don't you shoot one to cook it?"

Omar shook her head.

"They aren't worth it. Those black vultures are nothing but bone and feathers, and stink like rotten bodies. A gunshot will echo between the mountains forever if I fire the gun up here. It will carry down into the valleys, and they'll know we're here. To take that risk, we'd better have something worth shooting."

She suddenly stopped in her tracks to stare at me.

"Wait a minute. Did you just ask me why I didn't shoot one of those birds?"

I wagged my tail.

"Of course."

She cocked her head.

"Seriously? You can talk?"

I licked her hand.

"Only to those who can listen. But you're doing OK. You're making progress for someone who used to think that dogs were the Demon's spawn."

Omar shook her head.

"I must be going crazy. Here I am, on top of the mountain, starved to the core and frozen to the bone, and I hear dogs talk. Let's get out of here before it gets worse."

We did. We walked in silence for hours, then stopped to rest and shelter between the trunks of some spruce.

Omar gathered an armful of sticks and built a fire. It took her forever, giving more smoke than heat unless you stuck your nose close enough to get burned, but the flames were company. I squeezed so near that the smoke made me sneeze. Omar laughed.

"You know, Sadiq, it's not so much for the heat, though it's nice to warm your hands and dry your boots. But fire will keep away the Mountain Ghosts. The bears too. Any predator, in fact, since no animals like fires. The wolves, the sheep, and even the cats stay away. All but you. You're weird."

I chortled.

"I'm weird? Look at you. You're not a boy and not a girl; you ran away from home to go Dog knows where with just a dog for company. Isn't that weird?"

Omar nodded.

"Weird enough," she said, then remembered that she was talking to a dog and shook her head.

"We need another half day to cross the plateau, then we'll start going down. With some luck, we'll be out of the snow by tomorrow night. We may even find food. Keep your eyes peeled for rabbits, dormouse, or squirrels. And especially goats! If we got a goat, we'd eat for days."

Omar ate another handful of snow. I did, too, even though I hadn't eaten in so long that I was no longer hungry. Just weak and dizzy.

Omar took off his boots and held them by the fire.

"These were Father's boots, you know. Not his work boots — he wore those when he disappeared. These were his best boots, and the tunic and the coat were his best clothes. Mother adjusted them when I grew out of my clothes, and I've worn them ever since. They make me very happy. Whenever I wear his clothes, I feel caught in his hug. I hope he's watching us up there, and he'll put in a good word. We can use all the help we can get. I know he sees you and may wonder what I'm doing trekking across the mountains with a dog, but he won't get mad. He never does. He'll try to understand like he always did, and he'll see that you are nothing like the other dogs. You're special. I'll tell him all about you when we meet."

I shook my head.

"I'm sorry, Omar, but you're mistaken. In most ways, I'm just like all the other dogs. I may not be wired like Viper, athletic like Rambo, or even nosy like Lovely since I'm just an old golden retriever, but I'm still a dog. And whatever they told you about dogs is all wrong. Dogs aren't the devil's spawn. We are not evil. We never kill or even bite without a good reason. We live our lives guiding and protecting our humans to keep them out of trouble, and Dog knows it's not easy. So when you meet your father, tell him that dogs are nothing like your people make us out to be. We live to love and serve, and we never expect a reward. That should teach your humans something."

29

———————

Omar was right. After another freezing night, we crossed the snowy mountain plateau and headed down.

It got even harder. Clambering up those icy trails was a chore, but climbing down was a menace. The ice on the path had been sun-kissed just enough to be slippery-slick. Every step was a fight. I clawed the ice, struggling to hold my footing and stay away from the edge. My joints hurt, my legs shook, and my paws got numb with cold. Before too long, I got weaker than a newborn kitten.

Omar never relented.

She wrapped her turban around her boots to get a better grip on the ice and carved a walking stick out of an oak branch. She kept her hand on her gun and her eyes on the trail. And step by step, she headed down.

I watched her in wonder. How did this kid learn so much about the mountains? Where did she get the strength? With my four good paws and strong curved claws, I still slipped and needed breaks. She never did.

By the evening, we'd left the snow behind. Blades of thin grass squeezed between the dead leaves, their bitter juice a palate cleanser. Oaks and ashes lifted their green buds to the sky like tiny hungry fingers. The blistery wind turned into a breeze. Thank Dog. I may love snow, but spring means warmth and hope. But we ran out of water.

Omar dropped her bag in the little crevasse she'd chosen for shelter and loaded her gun.

"Don't worry, Sadiq. I bet we'll find a stream tomorrow and drink to our heart's content. Why don't you rest for a bit while I go look for food? You stay here and watch our stuff."

I yawned to disagree. I approve of food; I always approve of food. But where was Omar going, and why wasn't I going with her?

I sulked for a while, but the exhaustion overcame me, and I fell asleep. I was just sniffing the breeze with Rambo and congratulating Lovely on her new fancy collar when something woke me up.

I jumped to my paws and sniffed left and right. I listened. Nothing.

I lay my back down to catch another nap when something inside urged me to go find Omar. NOW.

I scrambled back to my feet, shook my head to chase away the fog, and started tracking Omar's scent. But I didn't get far. Her smell faded as I reached the cliff.

What the heck?

I sniffed left, I sniffed right, I even sniffed down, in the misty valley far below, but I got nothing. It was like she'd vanished into thin air, leaving no trace. But that couldn't be. There was nothing but a thousand-foot drop straight ahead and forbidding cliffs to both sides.

I retraced my steps.

There she is! I recovered her trail at the root of a tall oak tree leaning over the valley below. Omar's scent stuck to the trunk. I looked up, and sure enough, there she was, laying on her belly in the crook of a forked branch, fast asleep. The exhaustion had finally caught up with her. Her eyes were closed, but her hands were still on her weapon.

Should I wake her up or let her be? I wondered, when I saw a young ash tree shaking to my right. Something black crawled up, bending the slender white trunk, and I knew we had trouble.

I was still wondering what to do when the creature pointed his long, sharp muzzle to sniff Omar, and I went nuts.

"Omar! Wake up! Wake up! That...something is after you!"

Omar opened her eyes. She pushed herself up, but her hand slipped, and the branch moved. The other hand held the gun, so Omar tried to hug the branch with her legs but missed. She teetered over the cliff, ready to fall.

The black thing glared at me with his hungry yellow eyes, then glanced back at Omar, still struggling to hold on. Her right arm hugged the trunk, then her legs, and she melted into the tree like she was glued to it.

Black Blob turned to me.

The ash twisted and screamed as he leaped. He landed ten feet ahead of me, rolled to his paws, stood seven feet tall, opened his arms, and roared like thunder.

The mountains answered. I jumped back.

Whatever that was, it was taller than a grown man and twice as wide, with a shaggy coat, all black but for the white moon crescent on his chest. His tiny yellow eyes measured me. He sniffed, and his feral stench took my breath away.

Phew! I decided to skip the introductions. I'd never been less curious to meet someone. I stepped back, getting ready to run.

His massive paws sprouting hook-like claws longer than Omar's pesh-kabz reached to grab me. I yelped and tried to run, but my leg gave up.

I fell to my side and crashed to the ground. The thing leaped, reaching for my throat but barely missing it.

I rolled away and scrambled to my paws. Stinky growled with frustration and reached again, but I tucked my tail between my legs and dashed for my life. I only took three steps before his breath burned my neck.

I pushed with all I had and leaped away. Those fierce talons raked my back like a dozen daggers, from my neck to my tail, but he couldn't hold on. I darted forward, but his claws reached again and got caught in my collar.

I crumbled to the ground with a ton of stink on my back.

The shot rang.

His weight crushed me, and his yellow teeth grazed my shoulder. I tried to squeeze out, but he was too heavy. The red mouth roared, and the monstrous fangs reached for my throat.

I twisted, and he got the scruff of my neck instead. I yelped and raked his belly with my hind feet. He roared and went for my muzzle, ready to bite off my face.

I growled and went for his throat when a second shot shook the mountains. He fell limp.

I squeezed out from under him and spat out the stinky black fur.

Its frozen eyes stared at the sky, and a bloody foam came out of its mouth. The thing lay unmoving on its side.

Omar jumped down, holding her gun. She studied him and asked:

"Did you ever eat moon bear?"

My stomach flipped. I yawned and shook my head.

"Well, it's better than nothing."

30

It surely was. Omar sliced it thin, skewered it, and showed it the fire, and the bear turned out delicious. A bit chewy and still cold inside, but it was the best morsel I could remember. Especially after Omar dusted it with a pinch of salt from his bag.

"It's not tender like a spring lamb, but it's not bad for a bear kebab. The secret is the salt. Father always carried salt. Salt makes everything taste better, he said, even leaves or tree-bark soup — though not by much. If we were home, I'd dust it with some pepper and a little cumin and simmer it until it got tender. But we aren't home, and it's better than nothing."

I licked my lips and eyed another sizzling kebab.

"Are you kidding? This is the best bear kebab I've ever had. May I get another?"

I didn't mention that this was the only bear kebab I'd ever had — heck, it was the only bear I'd ever seen.

Omar smiled.

"There you are. You can have all you want — we can't take much with us. First, it's heavy, and second, it will spoil. It hurts me to leave it to the vultures, but I'll take all I can carry; I'll just smoke it a little. It makes it lighter and helps it keep better than raw."

She glanced longingly at the shaggy black skin stretched on the ground.

"I wish I could take the fur; it would come in handy in the cold. And the gall bladder. Chinese merchants pay good gold for Moon Bear's gallbladder; they think it heals everything, from red eye to cancer, but Father said that's nonsense. He said that the Chinese are infidels. They pray to...I forgot who they pray to, but it's not Allah, so they're infidels and unenlightened. Still, I wouldn't mind selling them the gallbladder, but I don't think we'll meet any Chinese where we're going."

She turned over the meat slices she'd skewered to smoke. I swallowed my last piece of bear and looked for another.

"Where are we going?"

Omar gave me another kebab.

"You know, Sadiq, it's hard to believe, but I really think I can hear you. Not like I used to hear Mother or Father, but it's like I feel your thoughts in my head."

"Sure you do. Like I do yours. I don't understand your words — I don't understand many words other than "Sit," "Stay," "Seek," and" Come." But I can smell your thoughts, hear the tone of your voice and know how you feel from the look in your eyes. That's better than words if you ask me. Humans can't talk to each other unless they speak the same language, and sometimes not even when they do. Hex that. You wouldn't believe how many times I've seen them fight and hate on each other because they don't understand one another. The dog way is better. Easier too, when you put your heart into it."

Omar shrugged. My bad. That was a lot for a beginner.

"Anyhow, we're heading to the Paki border. Pakistan has Taliban too, but at least they have a working government. That's what Uncle Aziz said before the Taliban shot him. They said he listened to the radio to un-Islamic things that were Haram. Mother cried and cried — he was her younger brother and only protector other than me — but that didn't bring him back. Anyhow. We'll head east through the mountains, then look for a place to cross into Pakistan. The problem is the fence. They say it's taller than two men standing on each other's shoulders and topped with coils of razor wire. Even worse, the Paki planted mines around it. But Uncle said they couldn't finish it since the Afghan Taliban didn't like it and kept pulling it down. We won't know until we get there if we got to the fence or a hole. Allah willing, we'll find a hole and get through. If not..."

She shrugged and went back to fussing with the meat. She turned it upside down so it dried on all sides, then looked up at the dark blue sky sprinkled with more stars than I could count.

"If we don't, we don't. At least we tried. You want more meat?"

Do I want more meat? Sure, I do. I always do. But after starving for a week, my stomach got queasy. A wave of nausea hit me, and I yawned.

"You're done, then? OK. Let's get some sleep. We want to be rested for tomorrow."

31

We curled back-to-back in our shelter to keep each other warm, but the morning chill woke me up. Outside the cave, the sun shone, the blue sky blushed pink, and countless birds sang like they had a mission.

Omar came out. Her breath puffed with steam. She rubbed her hands to warm them and smiled.

"Don't you love birdsong? Before the Taliban, we used to have a sweet-singing mountain nightingale. We kept it in a cage by the door and listened to its thrills for hours. But it wasn't just us. Every home in the village had a parakeet, a canary, or at least a cooing dove. But when the Taliban came, they said that the birds were a distraction from the only music that mattered — reading the Quran. And Allah intended birds to be free. They made us release them. But our birds had always been caged, so they didn't know how to fly. And they had nowhere to go. So they stayed there until the Taliban killed them with rocks."

Omar wiped her eyes with the back of her hand.

"I hated them for that. I still do. But it is what it is."

She packed the smoked meat and glanced longingly at the rest.

"Oh well. Let's go."

We headed down the muddy trail between fragrant cedars and moody pines, watching our steps on the rolling gravel. After a while, Omar stopped to listen.

"You hear that?"

"Hear what?"

"The water."

She was right. Somewhere to our right, beyond a thick hedge, there was water. We had to squeeze between prickly spruce and juniper bushes to find the river, but it was worth it.

A crisp stream sparkled, tumbling downhill, its gurgle better than music to my ears. We drank and drank until the water cleared the thickness from our mouths and softened our throats. Then Omar stripped off her brown tunic and wide shalwar kameez and walked into the stream. She shivered and laughed as the water, cold as snowmelt, ran over her slim body. I wondered how I ever thought she was a boy. Her short dark hair fell over her face, but her narrow waist and the swell of her chest were that of a girl. So was her bubbly laughter. How could I ever be so blind?

"Dog! Come," she gestured.

I followed her into the stream. The freezing water washed away pounds of grime from my coat and took years off my soul as we ran, laughed, and splashed each other.

"That was fun."

Omar panted and sat on a sunny rock to dry off. I came out, shook, and sprayed her all over. She laughed.

"Now I should go back and wash again, you dolt. Mother said that if the faithful touch a wet dog after washing for prayer, they must go back and clean themselves seven more times. And one of those should be with dirt. I wonder how dirt makes you clean. They must mean that even dirt is cleaner than you, filthy animals."

She roughed my ears and hugged me.

"Oh, dog, I love you. You're the best friend I've ever had. As a matter of fact, you're the only friend I've ever had. I never had someone I could tell whatever I thought without worry. Not Father,

Mother, or even Grandma, even though they loved me and would have done anything for me. But they would scold me and tell me how wrong I was. You never do."

I licked her nose.

"You just wait."

She wiped herself with the cloth of her turban and put on her clothes. Her smile vanished as if the world's weight landed on her shoulders.

"Time to go, Sadiq."

I shook, she grabbed her bag, and we started down the overgrown path by the stream. It looked abandoned, but a scent hit my nose and stopped me in my tracks.

"What?"

I sniffed up and down. The scent came from the ravine to our right.

I wagged my tail and pointed that way.

"There's something here."

"Like what?"

"Something. We need to check."

Omar shook her head, but she followed the path to the rocks on the ledge. It looked like nothing but a pile of stones until you found the curtain over the opening and smelled the need.

Omar sighed.

"We're supposed to avoid people, you know? Everyone we meet could turn us in to the Taliban."

I knew, but my instinct spoke louder than her words. We had to check this place, even though I didn't know why.

Omar shook her head.

"Ok then. I hope you aren't crazy."

She scrambled up the trail to the opening and pulled away the curtain. The sun peeked inside the windowless rock hut, lighting the dirt floor and the roof of flat rocks.

"How crazy is that? Listening to a dog?" Omar mumbled, but she went in. I followed.

Not much inside but a mattress, an empty water bucket, and a bag that smelled like potatoes.

"So, we're here why?"

Good question. I sniffed the darkness, looking for more. I found an opening and went to check it out when someone called.

"Who are you? What are you doing here?"

32

I froze. Omar readied her gun.

I lifted my muzzle and sniffed.

Female. Old. Hurting.

I stepped toward the opening.

"Don't!" Omar whispered.

I ignored her. She may have known her way around bears and snow leopards, but I was boss when it came to sniffing dark places. Because, unlike humans, I don't much use my eyes. Whenever things get hairy, I go by my smell and my instinct, and they've never been wrong.

The second room was barely big enough for a thin mattress covering the dirt from wall to wall, and the tiny old woman curled on it. Her sunken white eyes, jutting bone cheeks, and the messy tuft of gray hair made her look like an old bird. Her chest heaved with every painful breath. She was hurting, and she was no danger.

I growled.

"It's OK. Nothing to worry about."

The woman lifted her head.

"What was that?"

Omar stepped in, holding her gun. She saw the woman and dropped it.

"It's just me, Auntie. Are you sick?"

"Who are you?"

"I'm Omar."

"What are you doing here?"

"Just... hunting."

"Where are you from?"

The questions came fast and furious, and Omar struggled. Time to intervene.

"Something's wrong with her," I barked.

The woman's jaw fell.

"What was that? Is that a dog?"

Her eyes searched the room, then settled somewhere behind me. She was so blind that she couldn't see a big orange dog under her nose.

Omar shook her head in annoyance.

"What happened to you? Are you hurt?"

The woman tried to roll to her back but screamed in pain.

"I just sat on the mattress, and a terrible pain stabbed my hip. I couldn't walk after that. I couldn't even crawl out to get water."

"I'm sorry, Auntie. Let's see what we can do."

Omar brought her water bottle to the woman's lips and held her head. The woman drank and wiped her mouth.

"That was good, thank you."

"Let me look at your hip."

Omar pulled away the faded blue blanket. The old body underneath was only skin and bones, and her hip bone stuck out like an egg.

"You got your hip out of joint, Auntie. We'll have to put it back in, but it will hurt."

The woman snorted.

"What's new? When you get to be my age, everything hurts. Life hurts. Can you put it back?"

"I think so."

"How old are you?"

"Mom says I'm almost thirteen."

"How come you know how to put bones back? I'm almost seventy, and I don't."

"Father taught me. He was...he was a wise man."

"He's dead?"

"Yes."

"Why?"

"The Taliban."

"May Allah curse their worthless souls. They bring nothing but pain and destruction. So how are you going to do it?"

"First, I need you to lie on your back."

The woman tried to roll, but she yelled and fell back.

"Sorry, Auntie."

Omar rolled her. The woman screamed, and Omar let her catch her breath.

"Now what?"

"Now, we'll do it."

Omar turned the empty bucket upside down and sat it by Auntie's hip. She stepped on the bucket, grabbed the woman's leg, sat Auntie's knee over her own, then pushed her ankle down.

Auntie screamed. Something clicked. The egg vanished.

"Sorry, Auntie, I bet it hurts. I'll make you some willow-bark tea, and you'll feel much better."

"I feel better already. Thank you."

Omar made her tea and fed her our smoked bear. Auntie ate and drank, then got back to asking questions.

"Where are you going?"

"I'm...I'm looking for one of our sheep. It got lost on the mountain."

Auntie laughed.

"Don't lie to me, child. I may be blind, but I still can see through you. You ran away from home?"

Omar sighed.

"Yes."

"Why?"

"The Taliban wanted to lash me."

"Why?"

"They found out I'd played Father's rubab."

"That's it? So what? They wouldn't have killed you. Not if it was the first time. You ran away from home to escape a few lashes?"

Omar nodded.

"There's got to be more than that. You said your father died?"

"Yes."

"Who looks after your mom?"

Omar sighed.

"So there's no one left to look after your mom, but you ran away to escape a few lashes. That makes no sense. Unless...you're a Bacha Posh, aren't you?"

Omar's eyes grew big. She glanced at the door and grabbed her weapon, ready to leave.

Heavy steps crushed the gravel outside. It was too late to run.

"Mom?"

33

—————

The steps came closer.

"Mom? Are you here?"

"Don't tell him," Auntie whispered.

I squeezed to hide behind the potatoes as a bearded man blocked the light. His blue tunic and shalwar kameez were dirty and ripped, and his face was gray with fatigue, but his dark eyes were sharply awake as they slipped from Auntie to Omar.

"Who's this?"

"I'm..."

"He's Omar. He's my older sister's grandson. Omar, this is your uncle Abu-Zar."

Omar dropped to her knees and touched the man's hand to her forehead. The man frowned.

"I didn't know you had an older sister."

"She died long ago; Allah rest her soul. But she was a good woman. So's the kid."

Auntie told him how she suffered alone for days until Omar came to help. Abu-Zar's eyes softened. He thanked Allah for his mercy, then turned to Omar.

"Thank you for helping my mom. My home is your home. Whatever you need, I'll give you, and whatever I can do for you, I will."

He bowed. Good time to get lost, I thought, so I squeezed out quietly and sat outside the door. I'd better be out in the open when it's time to get lost.

"Thank you, uncle, but...."

Auntie cut her off.

"As a matter of fact, Omar came here to ask for help, Abu-Zar. He needs to cross the border."

Abu Zar's bushy eyebrows came together. He scratched his unkempt beard.

"Cross the border? Are you kidding? That's impossible."

"For other people. But for you...."

"Mother!"

"Are you refusing to help this kid? Your own nephew who saved your old mother from a fate worse than death? Do you know how it felt to lay here alone and in pain without help? I couldn't even get water."

"I'm sorry, Mother, but...."

"Three days, I tell you. I was alone for three whole days before Omar helped me."

"I'm sorry, Mother, but you know I had work to do. I came back as soon as I could."

"That's what I'm talking about. You cross the border all the time, but you won't help the blood of your blood, the son of your cousin...."

"But he's just a boy. What will he do there alone if he crosses the border? And what on earth does he need to cross the border for?"

"That's not your problem," Auntie said.

Abu-Zar shook his head.

"Sure, it is. If I'm helping him, it is my problem. And I tell you again, he won't make it alone. The border is a nasty place with terrible people. Who do you think crosses that border? Mullahs?

Schoolteachers? No. No one but people with something to hide cross that border, whether it's drugs, weapons, or some other contraband. Just look at him. He's pretty as a girl and so young he's beardless. Someone will grab him and sell him for his weight in gold. And those who buy him.... I don't even want to think about what they'll do to him. I want no part of this."

"I'm not alone," Omar said, her voice clear as a bell.

"What?"

"I'm not alone. Dog?"

"What?" I barked, sticking my nose through the door.

Abu-Zar's jaw fell.

"What the..."

"What is it?" Auntie asked.

"A dog. The kid's here with a filthy, God-cursed dog."

Auntie sighed.

"Merciful Allah be praised, my eyes are so bad I can't see my own hands, but I wish I could see that. Oh well. Omar, what's with the dog?"

"I...I stole it. And I'm going to sell it to make money."

Auntie shook her head.

"Really, Omar? Who do you think will pay money for a dog? Nobody wants them, filthy creatures."

"The Americans will."

They kept talking, but I didn't understand a thing, and I got bored. I lay my nose on my paws to catch a nap, and I must have slept for a while. When I opened my eyes, Omar was getting ready to go. She filled her water bottle, put it in her bag, grabbed her gun, and came out.

"Great help you've been, lying there snoring like a chainsaw while I tried to tell them you'd protect me if someone tried to snatch me. Abu-Zar thinks I'm nuts, but he agreed to take us. His mother shamed him into it. He said he'll take us to a hole in the fence. We should get there before sunrise."

I yawned.

"And then?"
Omar shrugged.
"Allah only knows."

34

———

We headed north as the sun went down. Omar and I followed Abu-Zar for hours over dusty trails that meandered up and down too many mountains to count. My paws got so tired I thought they'd dry and fall off. Even Omar, who never complains, looked peaked. But Abu-Zar didn't stop, didn't slow down, and never looked back. We saw nothing but his broad, bent back and the gun in his hand. I knew without sniffing that he couldn't wait to get rid of us.

We were climbing down yet another hill when I sniffed people coming. I growled to let Omar know.

"Someone's coming," she said.

Abu-Zar glanced at her.

"How do you know?"

"The dog smelled them."

Abu-Zar shook his head, but he looked around for shelter. There wasn't much but a few scraggly bushes scattered here and there over the orange dirt stretching as far as I could see. So we stepped off the path to melt into the ground, hoping that the darkness and the bushes were enough.

Just heartbeats later, two armed men loaded with backpacks

front and back emerged from the darkness heading to where we came from. We waited for them to disappear, then got moving.

Abu-Zar's mood had changed. He slowed to let us catch up and asked Omar, "Why are you crossing the border?"

"To run away."

"Why? What did you do?"

"I played my father's rubab, and someone told the Taliban."

"That's it?"

"That's why they killed my father."

Abu Zar sighed.

"I didn't think you had a chance, kid. I still don't. But maybe that dog isn't as useless as I thought if he can warn you about hidden dangers. Stay away from people — all the people — as best you can. Don't forget that the Paki mined the border on their side. They don't like folks to come and go as they please, so they planted thousands of mines along that fence. The Taliban took down the fence, but not the mines. An opium trafficker died only last week, and another one lost a leg. You sure you want to do this?"

Omar's lips trembled.

"I'm sure."

Abu-Zar shrugged.

"OK then. No skin off my back."

He kept going and going. Just when I thought I couldn't walk anymore, he stopped.

"See that there?"

"What?"

"The ridge. Up here, that's all that's left of that fence. That, and the mines. Some say they're scattered to fifty or a hundred feet beyond the fence, but nobody knows for sure. Once you pass that, you should be in the clear, but don't forget nobody here is your friend. Stay away from them all if you can. Good luck."

"But..."

"But what?"

"You're leaving us here?"

Abu-Zar shook his head.

"Are you kidding? You thought I'd hold your hand to help you cross the border? I don't know why you're doing it, and I think that's a bad idea. Still, I did what Mother asked me to. I brought you all the way here, even though I know she's lying. You're not my nephew because she never had an older sister. I'll take you back if you change your mind, but other than that, you're on your own."

Omar fell to her knees and touched the man's hand to her forehead.

"That you, Uncle.

Abu-Zar shook his head and left without looking back.

35

Omar's eyes were dark with worry as he watched Abu-Zar fade into the night. She turned to face the crumbly, steep, dirt bank to the top of the ridge and sighed.

"Let's go, Sediq."

The black sky started to fade as we crawled up the treacherous slope, struggling to keep our footing over rolling gravel and uneven terrain. The ridge wasn't far, but it was slow going. Still, for the first time ever, I was first. Up that abrupt hill, four feet worked better than two. If one slipped, you still had three left to keep you in business. Far behind, Omar struggled.

She leaned on her weapon, clutching the dirt and holding on to the spiny evergreens, to pull herself up the hill step by step.

I kept going, clawing my way up to the naked ridge. By the time I reached the top, the sky had turned pink.

I stopped to rest and look around. Nothing but crumbly orange dirt dotted with a few measly bushes stubborn enough to survive. No houses, no water, no place to hide.

I looked back at Omar. Her legs shaking, her face shining with sweat, she'd gotten halfway up the ridge, and she hung on to a bush for dear life.

I wagged my tail.

"Come on, Omar, you can do this. Just a few more steps, and you'll get here.

She mumbled something under her breath, then pulled herself up again. She fell to her hands and knees, dug her boots into the rolling dirt, and grabbed onto it with both hands. It took a while, but she made it to the top and let herself fall to the ground.

I licked the sweat off her face. It was salty, and it smelled like her. Omar laughed.

"Leave me alone, Dog."

"I can't. We need to go. The sun's almost up."

Omar sighed and crawled back to her feet.

"OK then. Let's go. Just watch out for those mines, will you?"

She started down the other slope, but I grabbed her tunic and held her back.

"Take it easy, girl. This is your lucky day. You happen to have a mine specialist right here. So now I go first, and you follow," I growled.

Omar didn't get it.

"What do you want?"

She needed explaining. So I got in her face, bared my teeth, and growled.

"I go first. You follow."

She shrugged.

"Whatever."

I headed down the other side of the ridge, sniffing every inch to clear our path. Omar followed. The sky had turned red, and the sun was almost up when I caught the first whiff of explosive.

I sat to point out the mine like I always did. Omar stared at me.

"What are you doing?"

I wagged my tail to explain.

"You check it, then you tell the others and give me my Kong," I wanted to say. But then I remembered that she didn't know how to check bombs and I didn't have a Kong.

So we moved to plan B. I gave the mine a wide berth and headed down the slope with Omar on my heels.

We'd cleared the mines by the time the sun was halfway up the sky, but I had no strength left. I fell behind.

Omar called.

"Come on, Sediq. We need to get moving. You heard Abu Zar — this is a bad place to hang out. We can't stop. We need to find water and shelter. Let's go."

I tried, but my paws felt like lead, my hips hurt, and my back ached. I struggled to shuffle, but I fell farther and farther behind until I couldn't go anymore. I dropped to the ground.

"You go ahead, Omar. I'll catch up with you later."

"You can't stay here. We need to go."

I wagged my tail to apologize.

"I'm sorry, Omar. I can't. You go."

"I can't go without you."

She picked me up and lifted me on her shoulders. She headed forward, stumbling under my weight. The sun bathed us in fire as she walked and walked until it hurt to sit on her shoulders.

Our shadow had shrunk to nothing when I finally smelled the forest far ahead. Omar saw it too.

"We'll get there, Sadiq," she said.

That's when I heard the engine noise.

36

———

A cloud of dust barrels upon us. Just heartbeats later, the jeep stops, and two men in brown uniforms point their guns at us.

"Drop the gun," the tall man says. He wears camouflage, like my soldiers.

One of the men in brown translates, and Omar drops her gun to the ground.

"Lay on the ground, face down."

Omar puts me down gently, then lets herself melt into the ground with a sigh.

"What the heck?"

The tall man stares at me like he's never seen dogs before. I sniff his way and wag my tail. Boy, am I happy to see him! I don't know him, but I know that uniform, the helmet, and the smell. He smells like shampoo, bubblegum, and stress sweat, just like the soldiers in our unit.

"Ask him what's with the dog."

Omar answers and the short man translates.

"He says it's an American military dog. The Taliban want him, but he brought him across the border so they can't get him."

The tall man stares at me. I stare back.

He slaps his thigh.

"Come here, boy. Come here!"

I wag my tail and sniff his hands, boots, and privates. They all check out.

He studies my tag. He takes his time with it, turning it this way and the other, whips out his phone to snap pictures, then makes a call.

"Yep, sir. Sergeant Scott here. I'm at the Durand Line, just north of Quetta. I'm here with the Paki border patrol. We were waiting for a delivery, but we stumbled upon a surprise."

He shakes his head.

"No, not any of the most wanted list. No, no Taliban either."

"I have a dog. Yes, a dog. It looks like a golden retriever. His name is Prozak. Yes, PROZAK. With a K. He's supposed to be a military dog in Afghanistan who somehow ended up with the Taliban, then escaped. Sure, I'll wait. Yes."

Sargent Scott's eyes go from me to Omar, and he tells the man in brown, "Check him out. Make sure he doesn't have a suicide vest and find out who he is."

The short man who chats with Omar must be a translator. We had them at the base. They helped our men communicate with the locals. Friendly folks, but terribly stressed since the Taliban hated them even more than they hated us. I could smell it in their sweat.

Sergeant Scott's eyes widen.

"Really? Five months ago, you said? That's unbelievable. I can't imagine where he's been all this time. I wish he could tell us. No, sir, he's not with his handler. He's here with an Afghan kid who carried him on his shoulders. Yes, we are gathering information right now. Sure, I will. I'll send you the pictures and let you know what we get out of the kid as soon as we get it. Of course, sir. We won't let him disappear. I understand it's a big deal, especially now. Sure, I'll keep you posted."

He slips the phone into his pocket and stares at me.

"Oh, boy, how I wish you could talk, Prozak. I'd die to know what happened to you and where you've been all this time. But maybe your friend here can shed some light, eh?"

He rubs my ears and turns to the translator.

"So? What does the boy have to say?"

The man grins from one ear to the other.

"No boy, sir."

"What do you mean?"

"There's no boy, sir. This is a Bacha Posh. She's a girl."

37

———————

"A what?"

"A girl, sir. She's a Bacha Posh that dresses in boy's clothes and lives like a boy so she can support her family, but she's not a boy."

Sergeant Scott shakes his head.

"Boy, girl, whatever. What did she tell you about the dog?"

"She found him fighting a snow leopard in the mountains."

"Fighting a snow leopard? This dog?"

"Yes, sir. She'd been stalking the snow leopard for weeks, but it always managed to escape. But since he was fighting with the dog, he didn't hear her, and she shot him dead."

"The leopard?"

The short man looks at him like he's feeble.

"Yes, sir. She didn't shoot the dog."

"I guess. And then?"

"The dog was wounded and had a broken leg. The girl took him to her home, hid him, and nursed him to health. But the Taliban were looking for him, so she was afraid they'd find him there and kill her entire family."

"And did they find him?"

"No, not the dog. But they found the rubab."

"The rubab?"

"Yes, sir. That's a musical instrument, a bit like a guitar. We play it at weddings and celebrations. The Taliban found it in her cave."

"She has a cave?"

"That's where she lives, sir. That's her home. Her folks are too poor to live in a house, so they found this cave…"

"Never mind the cave. What's with this rubab?"

"That's a musical instrument, sir. And it's banned by the Taliban because they say the faithful shouldn't waste time with the music; they should pray to Allah instead. So, when they found the rubab, she knew they would sentence her and her mom to lashes. But she was afraid they'd find out she's a girl and kill her."

"Kill her? Just because she's a girl?"

"No, sir. Because she shows her face and walks unaccompanied and lives like a boy. That's a terrible crime in the Taliban's book, and she thought they'd kill her."

"So?"

"So, she ran away and took the dog with her. They traveled for weeks to get to the border. And there they are."

"I see."

He doesn't smell like he sees. He smells about as confused as they get, but he turns to Omar and bows.

"That you for saving this dog."

Omar smiles.

"He saved me just as many times."

"I applaud your bravery and appreciate your taking care of Prozak. But it's time he gets back to his people. We'll take him to the vet to have him checked, and we'll take good care of him from now on. Thanks again for looking after him."

"And me?" Omar asks.

"The Paki authorities will look after you in conformity with their rules. I'm sure you'll be safe and comfortable, and I wish you all the best."

"But…the dog?"

"We'll look after the dog, don't worry. You take care of yourself."

He grabs my collar and pulls me into the jeep.

Omar looks at me with tears in her eyes. I want to run and lick away her tears, but Sergeant Scott holds on to my collar, and the jeep gets moving.

I watch Omar grow smaller and smaller, and my heart aches.

We've been together through so much. From the day she saved me from the cat to today, when she carried me on her shoulders to get us both to safety, she's been there for me.

I've been there for her too. From saving her from the bear to avoiding the bomb she was going to step on, I did my best to keep her safe and make her feel loved.

And now she's gone. Just like that, I'm speeding away in this jeep and leaving her behind.

I'm heartbroken, but I'm too exhausted to fight.

I fall asleep and wake up as they take me to someplace that smells like the vet. I get the full vet treatment — microchip check, blood draw, flea bath, tick check, and the other horrible things vets do when they get their paws on you. By the time they lock me in a crate, I'm too tired to live.

I fall asleep and dream of Ruby.

38

I lie on the grass, waiting for Ruby's bus like I do every day. It's hot, and I could use some shade, but I don't move because I know she needs me here.

She never complains, but I smell her sorrow whenever she returns from school. She jumps out of that bus like it's on fire.

There it is. The red lights flash, and I rush to the end of the driveway, wagging my tail. The door opens, and Ruby comes out, her short purple hair blown by the wind, her eyes looking for me.

I bark hello, and she hugs me and gives me her pack. I drag it and drop it on the porch as Ruby hugs Father. He kisses her hair.

"How was your day, sweetheart?"

"Just fine."

She smiles, but I know she's lying.

Father doesn't. Not until she bursts into tears. But then he hugs her like he wants to keep the world away.

"What happened, sweetheart?"

Ruby shrugs.

"Same old, same old. But I'm just tired of it."

"Of what?"

"The kids. They act like I'm a mutant. They laugh behind my

back and stare at me when I'm not looking. Then I get these notes...."

"What notes?"

"Like this."

She hands him a folded piece of paper. He adjusts his glasses and reads:

"You're an abomination. You're not a normal girl, and you're not a boy, no matter how much you'd like to be. We don't need losers like you here. Why don't you jump and drown in the pond? Or shoot your brains out with your stupid father's gun if you really want to make the world a better place?"

Father turns white. He swallows hard, folds the paper, and puts it in his pocket.

"That's awful, Ruby. Horrible, harmful, and stupid. Is this the only one?"

Ruby shakes her head.

"No. But this is the worst one because it comes from Melissa."

"Your Melissa? Your best friend? What makes you think that?"

"I recognize the paper. It's from her father's stationery."

Father shakes his head.

"I can't believe this. It has got to be a mistake. Let me work on it."

"There's nothing you can do."

"Sure, I can. I'll go see the principal."

"The principal won't do anything. He never does."

"But he needs to know!"

"He knows. He's seen them mock me over and over and never said anything. I think he's pleased."

"That's impossible. The principal can't condone bullying! I will..."

"Trust me on that, Father. I know you love me and you want to help. If there were anything you could do, I'd ask you. But there isn't. I am who I am, and..."

"You are a wonderful, caring, beautiful human being, Ruby.

There's nobody like you. Remember what your mother said: You can do whatever you want to do, and be whatever you want to be, if only...."

Ruby sighs.

"Mother's dead, Father. And everyone but you thinks I'm an abomination that doesn't deserve to live. Even Melissa. She's no longer talking to me. She got in with the hot girls, and they all laugh at me. They don't even try to hide it. They want me to hear."

She runs in and slams the door, and I wake up.

I'm not at home. I'm in the kennel, and this all happened forever ago. It's been years since I lost Ruby. Now, it's Omar.

39

───────

The following days were a blur. I dreamed about Ruby every night and waited for Omar every day. But she never came.

Like that wasn't bad enough, they fed me nothing but kibble. Chicken and barley. Pathetic! I hadn't had kibble since the base, Dog knows how long ago, and it hadn't gotten any better in the meantime. I longed for bear kebabs and rice with mutton bones, but I only got kibble. Phew!

I left it sitting there and lay my nose on my paws, waiting for Omar.

Was she coming to get me or what?

She didn't.

So I spent my days remembering the fight with the cat, Omar shooting the bear, and our journey across the mountain, day after day of empty stomachs and frozen feet. I remembered playing in the snow, bathing in the river, and Omar carrying me on her shoulders.

She cared about me; I knew she did. She had to come and get me, didn't she?

But she didn't.

I started wondering if something had happened to her, like to

Cho. And Ruby. Or if she forgot about me....

Then one day, they loaded my crate on a truck, then on a plane. The place I landed smelled like gasoline, cut grass, and fried food. It smelled like home.

I waited between boxes and coffers in my crate until a short soldier with thick round glasses gawked inside.

"Prozak?"

I wagged my tail. I didn't know him, but he knew me. And he smelled OK. Better than OK, I thought, when he slipped me a slice of beef jerky through the grates.

"I'm Walter. Corporal Sullivan, in fact, but you can call me Walter. I hope it's OK if I call you Prozak? I know I should call you Sir since you're a sergeant and all, but I hope we'll be friends. I wonder how you became a sergeant. What did you do? No matter what I do, I'm still a corporal. But never mind. I've been assigned to you, you know, kinda like your personal assistant. I'll look after you, feed you, and take you for walks. That's all good and fun, but I'm also supposed to organize your appointments, you know. Like you have a dozen of them just next week. See this?"

He flipped through some papers and got one to show me.

I sniffed it. It smelled like paper.

"That's your schedule. You're going to meet all sorts of important people. Someone from Defense, then the groomer. We might go to the Pentagon on Wednesday if they find a free slot in your schedule. I've never seen such a busy dog. Sorry, I meant to say K-9. You don't mind if I call you a dog, do you?"

I wagged my tail politely, but I was getting antsy. My last appointment with a patch of grass had been forever ago, so I was growing impatient. Walter understood.

"I get it. I'm sorry it took so long. Now we're waiting for a call from transport. They'll take us to the kennel. I'll let you know as soon as...there it is."

"Yep. Sullivan here. We're waiting for you. Half an hour? Are you kidding? We can't wait another half an hour. We need to go now. What? Whatever. Call me when you get here."

Walter shook his head and slipped the phone into his pocket.

"Half an hour! Are you kidding me? Let's go."

He opened my crate and clipped his leash to my collar.

"Just act like you own the place, will you? Keep your nose up and don't look at anyone until we find the grass."

That was easy since I was in a hurry. We cut through the crowds like nobody's business. I didn't even stop to bark at the Siamese in an orange cat carrier on the carousel.

We slipped through the door and found a patch of dirt under a scraggly little tree so ugly it looked fake.

"What do you think? I know it's not grass, but...."

What did I think? I lifted my leg and showed him what I thought. Walter laughed.

"Not fussy, are you? That's good, since we have a lot of work to do, starting now. We'll stop to see Colonel French on our way to the kennel. He wanted to see you first, since you're such a hero and all over the news and everything. Colonel French is very important. He heads the committee for...I forgot what committee, but I know it's important, so we'd better be on our best behavior. Don't pee on his carpet, and don't bite him, OK?"

I wagged my tail.

"I'm good for now."

The truck arrived, and we got on our way.

Colonel French's office was high up in a tall building, so we took the elevator. The humans turned up their noses and got out when we got in.

Walter shook his head.

"What a bunch of sissies! I'd like to see how they smell after spending 24 hours locked in a crate."

I wondered what he meant, but not for long because we got to Colonel French's secretary, and she took us to the great man himself.

He sat at a massive desk with his back to the window. I wondered how he watched the squirrels. But he didn't. He only watched the papers on his desk.

I sniffed the carpet. Disinfectant. But the room smelled like coffee, stress sweat, and Glade freshener. I was going to check the plant in the corner to see if it was fake when the colonel raised his head. He glanced at Sullivan, then looked at me.

"Is this it?"

"This is K-9 Prozak, sir. I'm Corporal Sullivan."

Colonel French's steel eyes moved from my ears to my toes and back.

"After all the fuss they made about him, I thought he'd be bigger. More imposing. But it is what it is. And as a matter of fact, the smaller and more ragged he looks, the more impressed they will be."

"Who, sir?"

"Everyone. Those who think he's a huge deal. 'The heroic K-9 who escaped the Taliban and found his way home.' If you thought the fuss the Taliban made when they took him was bad, you haven't seen anything yet. This dog will be in every newspaper and magazine in the world and all over TV. I don't care for dogs — I'm a cat man myself — but this is good PR. And God knows we need it after the withdrawal debacle. OK. Make sure he's healthy. Teach him some manners if he forgot them while he ran wild in the mountains. And keep me posted on his appointments. He doesn't go anywhere and doesn't meet anyone without my say-so, got it?"

"Yes, sir."

"And give him a bath. He stinks."

40

———

Walter was right. I had never been so busy. Not even when I sniffed the desert for IEDs. My partners and I still had time to chill in the evenings when the soldiers played cards and chatted at their end of the hangar. We K-9s napped, cleaned our tails, and sniffed the breeze.

Oh, how I missed them! Rambo and Lovely were my pack. I was always there for them, and they were always there for me. And all they expected from me was to be myself. Even the soldiers wanted nothing else once I'd cleared our way through the desert and checked the compounds for explosives.

But these people? They're weird.

The whole day, they line up to take photos. I can't lift my leg to a bush without someone snapping a picture. After I get groomed, it's a mob scene. And still, it's never enough.

"Can you make him look more fierce?" a young woman asked Walter.

"More fierce?"

"Yes. Like he's about to attack. Can you make him wrinkle his nose, flash his teeth, and growl to look scary?"

"But why?"

"Well, he's supposed to have crossed the Afghan mountains on his own. Fought wild beasts. Escaped the Taliban. Whatever. He should look scary; he shouldn't look like a pet."

Walter shook his head.

"Ma'am, he looks like he looks. He did whatever he did, looking just like this. Now, if you don't like it..."

"No, no. I'll take whatever I can get," the woman said, snapping so many pictures the flash made me dizzy.

"How about a nice romantic picture for a women's magazine? Can you make him hold a rose in his mouth?"

"Hold a rose in his mouth? What for?"

"It would make a fantastic picture. I bet that could get me the cover. Can we tuck it behind his ear if he can't hold it?"

"Sorry, ma'am. Nobody touches K-9 Prozak, and nobody gives him anything. No props."

"But why? What sort of marketable pictures can you get with a dog who doesn't even do any tricks?"

Walter turned red. His glasses fogged, and his mouth zipped into a line.

"Sorry, ma'am. Those are the rules. I didn't make them."

"But why?"

Walter lowered his voice to a whisper.

"Ma'am, we got info that the Taliban is still looking for him. K-9 Prozak's escape made them lose face. Getting outwitted by a dog made them look like a bunch of fools. That's why they're still after him. They'd stop at nothing to destroy him and show the world their power. That's why we need to protect Prozak at all times."

The woman's face lit up like a Christmas tree.

"Wow! I didn't think about that! Now that's a story! Can I quote you on that?"

"I'm afraid not. I'm just a low-ranking soldier, and I'm not entitled to speak for the army. But maybe you could keep the source anonymous...."

"Great idea. Thank you so much."

Like that wasn't bad enough, I had to have photo ops with all sorts of officials, and they weren't any easier.

"Make sure the focus is on me, not the dog," Colonel French said. "This picture makes me look fat. And the dog is too big. Make it look smaller."

Walter didn't like it one bit.

"I'm sorry, Prozak. Sorry about all this. But it should be over soon. They're all so excited you managed to escape and make it back that they just can't get enough of you. But I bet it's gonna be over in a week or two, and you can go back to...What would you like to go back to?"

What would I like to go back to? Darned if I know. Anything but here with these silly humans where everything is so fake. Up in the mountains with Omar? That can't be. She had to flee, and she couldn't go back. Back home with Father and Ruby? That can't be either. I don't know where Father disappeared to, but Ruby.... How about Rambo?

"Can I go back to Kandahar to search for IEDs?"

Walter's face darkened, and he looked away. When he finally answered, he smelled defeated.

"I'm sorry, Prozak. I don't think you can. You see, when you were up there in the mountains, trying to escape, we...we left Afghanistan."

I cock my head, trying to understand.

"What do you mean we left Afghanistan? Kandahar too?"

Walter nods.

"So then where... where are they? The men in our unit? The lieutenant? Dan? And my buddy Rambo? Where are they?"

Walter shrugs.

"I don't know, Prozak. But I know that no man was left behind. Every one of our soldiers made it out. Some are back here, some in Germany or Qatar, but they're all safe."

That's something, at least. Safe is good, no? Even if it's boring. But...

"How about the dogs?"

Walter's face crumples.

"That's...that's complicated. Apparently, some dogs — only those that didn't belong to the army — could not be evacuated. There just wasn't enough room on those planes, you see. All the people who needed to get out...and the Taliban chasing them...."

"So, where are they?"

Walter sighs.

"I don't know, Prozak. I don't know where they are. But thinking about them keeps me up at night."

41

———————

Walter was wrong. The following week didn't get any better, nor did the one after that. If anything, it got worse.

The magazines ran their course, and so did the photo-ops, but the TV people went crazy.

"I don't know what to do. I've got eighteen requests for you this week. Eighteen! How crazy is that? There's CBN, ABS, SBC, and God know who else besides local stations in North Dakota, Vermont, and Minnesota. Then there's the Animal Welfare Society, the Alliance for Military Dogs, the K-9 Rescue Association, and others I forgot. So many I don't know what to do. I'll ask Colonel French.

Colonel French rubbed his hands.

"Excellent! That's even better than I hoped for. How many shows can he do a day?"

"But sir..."

"What?"

"That's hard for him. The lights, the noise, the people, and everything else. It's stressful. The photo ops weren't easy, but this? He's just an old military dog, and he's tired. After all he's been through..."

"Oh, come on, Sullivan. He's just a dog! He doesn't understand and doesn't care! And if he does, so what? It's not like he's doing anything better! We need PR now more than ever. After that debacle of a retreat, we must show the world that our military is still the best! Our men, our equipment, even our dogs. We need to show what we're made of."

He started pacing, speaking so loud that his secretary popped her head in to see what had happened.

"This is bigger than this dog. It's bigger than you and even me. This is about our army, our country, and how the world views us. The dog has to do what the dog has to do. He'll do his job."

Walter took me to one show after another. I watched humans I had never met acting like my best friends, even those who smelled of hate and fear and didn't want to touch me. I spent day after day listening to them speak words I couldn't understand because even after all this time, I still don't get words. What speaks to me are smells, touch, and heartbeats.

That got me really, really tired.

It was like that day, long ago, when I got too exhausted to walk, and Omar carried me on her shoulders. But now, she wasn't here to hold me. And it was a different kind of tired.

That time my paws were tired, but my heart had hope. I hoped we'd get through to where the Taliban was no more and Omar was no longer in danger. We'd stop walking and find a cave to live in like dogs and humans always did.

But now it wasn't like that. My legs were OK, but my heart was drained. I felt empty spending my life with people making no sense to do things I didn't understand. I had no pack, no purpose, and no friends other than Walter.

He tried to help me.

We did a Dogathlon with the Society for Homeless Animals. They wanted a show to make people send money to get food and find a home for homeless animals.

Walter's face lit up.

"You've got to do your best for this, Prozak! Just think about all the dogs, cats, goats, and ferrets who need a good home."

I cocked my head.

"I'm good with the dogs. Goats too. They're yummy. But cats? You can't be serious. They're evil!"

Walter shook his head.

"Come on, Prozak! You can do this! When people see how brave and handsome you are, they'll send oodles of money to help the homeless animals! I'm so proud of you!"

What could I say? Cats or not, I did my best. I wagged my tail, I barked, and I tried to look happy watching a dozen humans answer phones for the money to come in. It was exhausting, but they were thrilled.

Walter hugged me.

"What a wonderful job you did, Prozak! I'm so proud of you!"

The skinny woman who ran the show agreed.

"Yes, wasn't he wonderful? That was amazing! We couldn't have done better if we had Betty White helping us! Your Prozak is gold," she said, checking the numbers on the screen.

I lay my nose on my paws, looking forward to my crate.

Walter scratched his head.

"You know, I wonder..."

"What?

"Could you find Prozak a nice family to love him, take him for walks, and play with him? Someone who'd always be there for him?"

Skinny's jaw fell.

"Are you kidding? If we get him adopted, we won't see another cent! Our whole point is to show people how hard it is for an animal to find a home. Once he's adopted, it all goes poof! He needs to be the face of our cause, or he's useless. Just think about all the animals that he'll help get homes for."

"But he's old and tired, and he needs rest. This is hard on him, and I don't know how long he can keep doing it."

Skinny shrugged.

"Then let's make the most of it now. Do you have another slot for us next week?"

Walter didn't give up. He spoke to Colonel French.

"I'm worried about Prozak, sir. He doesn't look well."

The colonel glanced at me over his glasses.

"He looks fine to me. What's wrong with him?"

"He's tired. Depressed, I think. He doesn't eat well, and he doesn't even enjoy walking or playing with his Kong like he used to do. I'm afraid all this is too much for him."

"So what do you want me to do? Take him to the vet."

"I did. The vet said he's fine, but he's not. I know it. I'm afraid something terrible will happen if we don't do something."

"Like what?"

"Find a family to adopt him?"

The colonel glared at Walter like he had peed on his rug.

"Are you nuts? This dog is a national figure. He represents the army and even the United States. And you want to hand him to some...family to live in their kitchen and play with their kids? No way."

"But sir, what if he dies?"

The colonel shrugged.

"As a matter of fact, that's not a bad idea. The dog has run his course. He did what he had to. But going on, he's bound to get us embarrassed somehow. We'd have to manage the press, though. I wonder if we should blame it on the Taliban or if that would actually help their PR. Let me think and keep him alive in the meantime. Another week or so?"

42

Day after day, the show goes on.

Walter takes me to some new circus every day, then locks me back in my crate for the night. And I love it because when I sleep, I'm never alone. In my dreams, I patrol with Rambo, escape with Cho, or eat bear kebabs with Omar.

But more often than not, I'm with Ruby.

I dream about the last time we camped. We walked at sunrise, breathing the morning mist of the river; we napped in the grass, soaking up the sun; then lay in the tent and studied the evening sky. Well, Ruby did. I watched the fireflies zoom under my nose and snapped to catch them, but Ruby held me back.

"Leave them alone, Zak. Aren't they pretty? You'll kill them if you chomp on them. Can't you watch them without trying to catch them?"

"Not if they keep provoking me," I growled, then snapped as another one flew and almost touched my nose. But I missed it.

"Why don't you watch the stars then? See them up there? Daddy said we each have a star. Our soul flies up to it when we die and lives there forever. I wonder which one's mine."

I looked up. The stars were too many to count, but at least they stayed put. Not a single one flew by my nose like those darn bugs.

"See that one there? The one that blinks red? I think I'll take that one if they let me choose."

I tried to find it, but they all looked the same to me. I lay my nose on my paws to catch a nap, but Ruby was on a roll.

"And the small blue one to its left? I'll keep it for you, so we can be together."

I didn't know what she meant. But now, whenever I see the stars, I look for the one blinking red, and I wonder if she's still there. Then I look for the small blue one, wondering if she has saved it for me like she promised.

But I never find them.

And it's been so long.

43

"Today's show is something special," Walter said, brushing my ears until I thought they'd fall off. I snapped at him to leave me alone, and I tried to squeeze back into my crate, but he caught me by the tail and held me back.

"OK, OK, I'll let you be. Still, they said to get ready for a major surprise. They have something special for you."

That got me thinking. Something special? A chew bone, maybe? But I bet it's just another bandana.

They sometimes give me gifts, but they're all useless. Like what do I do with a bandana? Nothing! Those things are worse than useless; they're annoying, and they make it hard to scratch your neck. The collar does too, but at least that helps take your humans out on their leash. As for those rancid rawhide chews that turn all mushy on you? Disgusting! Now give me a fresh marrow bone...

"A marrow bone, you think?"

Walter shrugged.

"I don't think so. I doubt they'll want grease smeared all over the studio. This is BCX, a big TV network. They only interview celebrities, but they want you! What do you think?"

I shook.

"I'd rather go for a walk."

"Me too. But you know what? I'll take you for a walk afterward. And I'll try to get you a marrow bone tomorrow, OK?"

What could I say? We went.

The studio was another one of those places with glass tables, low sofas, and a dozen cameras watching my every blink. And a skinny blonde with smiling red lips and unreal white teeth who smelled worried.

I wondered what she worried about. After all, she didn't have to put up with the cameras watching her clean her privates. Nor wonder if lifting her leg at the artificial grass was OK.

I hadn't finished wondering when a hundred lights went on, and she said:

"Good evening, everyone. Welcome to our show. We have an exceptional guest tonight. Cute too! Please, give a hand to our hero, K-9 Prozak!"

The speakers clapped so loud they shook the walls, but I was used to it by now. I didn't even jump; I just blinked away the lights in my eyes and wagged my tail left.

"Dear Prozak, we're so glad you're here tonight. We have a tremendous surprise for you. Look who's here to see you."

I looked, but with those lights in my eyes, I could see nothing but shadows. So I sniffed like one does.

What? It can't be!

I sniffed again.

"Prozak?"

"Omar? Is that you?"

I cried like a baby and jumped to hug her. She dropped to her knees and hugged me back, her eyes full of tears.

"I thought I'd never see you again," she said, wiping her tears with the back of her hand.

"Me too, me too!"

I barked and squeaked, and jumped on her until I knocked her over; then I licked her face, ran around like a puppy, and tried to jump out of my skin. But it was attached, so I just shed a bunch.

"How are you? I'm so glad to see you!"

She was. I smelled it and saw it in her laughing eyes. But she had changed. Gone were the dirty turban, the brown tunic, and the wide shalwar kameez smelling like smoke and sheep. Omar was dressed in ripped jeans and a t-shirt, and she smelled like soap and shampoo, just like Ruby. She even looked like her, with her smoky eyes and out-of-bed short hair. She could do with brushing, I thought, and I wondered if Walter had brought the brush.

Red lips wiped her dry eyes.

"What a lovely reunion. To all our viewers, this is Omar, the young Afghan woman who helped Prozak escape and saved his life. But she told us that he also saved hers, more than once. Together, just the two of them, they crossed the harsh Afghan mountains and evaded the Taliban. She took care of him when he was wounded and carried him on her shoulders when he was too tired to walk. As you can see, he didn't forget.

"To hear every detail of their incredible story, tune in tonight at nine for our full interview with Omar. She'll give us insights into the Afghan women's lives under the Taliban. She'll tell us about Prozak's fight with a snow leopard, how he helped Omar escape a black bear, and their arduous journey to freedom. Thank you all for watching."

The lights went off. Red-lips sighed with relief.

"Nice job, you two. You did great. I bet our ratings will go through the roof tonight. Omar, thank you for coming. Corporal Sullivan, you can take Prozak."

My hackles went up.

"Take me? Take me where?"

Walter blew his nose and clipped his leash to my collar.

"We're going back, Prozak."

"We're going back? But Omar?"

Walter turned to Red-lips.

"Omar needs to return to her foster home. Her status is still being processed. It will take the government a while to make a decision, but the bureau of children and families takes good care of her in the meantime. Don't they, Omar?"

Omar nodded. She wiped her tears and hugged me, then left with two women who waited for her. I tried to follow, but Walter held me back.

I went nuts.

"Wait! Wait! Omar! Where are you going? Take me with you! Don't leave me here!" I barked.

Omar looked back.

"Bye, Prozak. I'll miss you."

And just like that, she was gone. I was alone again.

I cried that night when Walter locked me in my crate. He did too.

"I'm so sorry, Prozak. But I'll find her for you. You just wait."

44

———————

I waited and waited, but nothing happened. Nothing but more and more shows with no Omar.

Then I got sick.

I didn't hurt, but I got really tired. And I stopped eating.

When I got too tired to do the shows and too weak to walk, Walter took me to the vet. She checked me every which way, then shrugged.

"I don't know what to say. His heart sounds fine, and his lungs too, but he looks bad. And he's lost a ton of weight. Truth be told, poor Prozak is an old dog, and he's had a rough life. I don't know if we can do much, but let's try to change his food and see what happens."

They switched me from kibble to cans and changed the cow on the bag to a lamb.

It still tasted like cardboard, and I got even weaker.

The vet shook his head.

"He doesn't look good. Why don't you feed him whatever he'll eat?"

Walter bought a cheeseburger, but the smell of it turned my stomach, and I puked.

Walter cried.

"You've got to eat, Prozak. You've got to eat, or you'll die."

I didn't eat.

Prozak took me to Colonel French.

"K-9 Prozak can't do any more shows, sir. He's not well. He does nothing all day but sleep. The vet thinks he'll die soon."

Colonel French shrugged.

"Oh well. At least we made the most of it while we had him. If he dies, he dies."

"But, Colonel, think about the publicity. The news. The newspapers. Social media. 'Prozak, the K-9 hero who defeated the Taliban, dies, abandoned by the army.' 'The bomb dog that survived the Afghan mountains can't survive the U.S. Army care.' 'After abandoning hundreds of dogs in the Kabul airport, the army manages to kill the only one who made it home on his own.'"

The colonel's mouth zipped into a line.

"What are you saying, Corporal?"

"It would be bad PR to have Prozak die in our care, sir."

The colonel scratched his head.

"You do have a point. Why don't you get him adopted, then? If he dies, he dies, but nobody can say it was our fault."

Walter's eyes sparkled with glee behind his thick glasses.

"Yes, sir."

He saluted, ready to leave.

"Corporal?"

"Yes, sir?"

"You can't adopt him. You're part of the army, and if he dies in your care, it's just like he died in the army. Find someone else. A former handler or some stranger."

"But sir..."

"No 'but.' Dismissed."

The joy seeped out of Walter like water from a leaky bowl. I wished I could help, but I was too sad and too weak. And I didn't know how.

And I didn't want to get adopted. The only dog I knew who got adopted was my buddy Viper, who retired, and I've never seen a more miserable dog. He'd rather they put him to sleep.

But Walter didn't give up.

"I'll find you the right human, Prozak. I wish I could take you, but you heard what the colonel said. And I know you want to be with Omar, but she doesn't have a home, so she can't take you. But I promise I'll get you the right human. They'll love you, and they'll find a way for you to see her."

I was too tired to listen, so I put my nose on my paws and fell asleep.

45

———————

Days came and went, and nothing happened. Like, really nothing: no photo-ops, no TV shows, and no more Colonel French.

I lay daydreaming in my crate until Walter took me for a short walk — I was too weak to walk far. Then he brought me back, and I slept and dreamed of my friends.

Until the day Walter smelled different. He was so excited his glasses fogged.

"Guess what?"

"What?"

"I have a surprise for you."

I sighed.

That's what he said every day. He tried to feed me this, that, or the other, but my stomach didn't want food. My heart either.

"No, really. Just wait. You'll love this one."

I wagged my tail left.

"Sure."

We went for our daily walk to the park across the street from the kennel. We sat on the grass and waited.

Nothing happened.

I was falling asleep when somebody's steps woke me up. A tall man with dark-rimmed glasses crossed the street, and his stride felt familiar.

"Corporal Sullivan?" he asked.

But he didn't glance at Walter. He looked at me.

His voice stirred something in me, and I lifted my nose to sniff his way.

"Prozak? How are you doing, old boy?"

I sniffed again.

"Father?"

The past barged in and turned me inside out. My heart swelled with fierce love and terrible sorrow.

I hadn't seen Father since the morning I found Ruby hanging from the lamp.

I smelled death, so I yelped and howled and barked. Father rushed in. He turned white and wailed, then ran to get a kitchen knife and cut her down. He lay her gently on the floor and called the ambulance, then fell to the ground.

I ran from one to the other and licked their faces. I tried to wake them up, but I couldn't.

The ambulance came and took them. I tried to follow, but they locked me in.

So I waited for them to return, though I knew Ruby wouldn't. I smelled it, I saw it in her frozen eyes, and I heard it in the silence of her heart.

But I waited.

They didn't.

Someday a man I didn't know opened the door. He looked at me with hard eyes and pursed his lips like it was my fault I couldn't go out, then dropped me at a kennel.

Still, I waited. I'd been to the kennel before, and they always came back for me.

Not this time.

Still, I waited.

Then the border patrol took me away, and I started training. I learned to sniff for drugs, counter-band, and even people. They gave me a handler, a job, and a home. I met my friend Jinx.

Somewhere along the way, I stopped waiting. But I never forgot.

And now Father was back.

I wished I could jump and hug him to tell him how happy I was, but I was so weak I fell over. So I just lay there and wagged my tail.

"I'm so glad you're back."

Father kneeled by my side.

"Oh, Prozak, it's been so long. I never thought I'd see you again! When they finally let me out of that hospital, I looked for you everywhere, but I couldn't find you. My brother said you had run away, but I think he lied. When I had my heart attack, I bet he thought I'd die, and he got rid of you. But I found you! And you look just the same seven years later."

I wagged my tail.

"You too. Sort of. Almost."

But he'd changed a lot. The Father I used to know was patient and kind. This one smelled bitter and lonely.

That made me so sad I had to lick his nose.

"It's good to see you. I still love you, you know. And I haven't forgotten."

Father's eyes filled with tears as he roughed my ears like he used to, and I could tell he missed Ruby and the happy times we had together.

I wagged my tail.

"I miss her too."

I wished I could tell him that our Ruby was up in the sky, waiting for us on her red blinking star, and she made reservations for us to join her. But it was too complicated, so I licked his tears and listened to his heart slow down instead.

After a while, he turned to Walter, who studied a garbage truck to give us privacy.

"Thank you for calling me, Corporal. I'd do anything to take Prozak back."

"There isn't much to do, sir. Just a bit of paperwork. And..."

"And?"

"Can I come to visit Prozak once in a while?"

46

Father's new home was a tiny blue bungalow at the northern edge of the town. It had a short driveway overgrown with lilac bushes and a mailbox the neighborhood dogs left their peemails on. That's how I found out that the house across the street belonged to Bolt, a retired Greyhound with a bad hind leg, and the one next door to a new mom: an expectant chocolate Lab named Cookie.

Compared to my crate and the Afghan's caves, Father's house was humongous. It had four rooms, a kitchen, and a basement. Even better, it had a sweet-smelling white porcelain bowl with fresh water, a sofa perfect for shedding, and a fridge complete with strips of bacon. It even had a doggie door in the back.

I sniffed every inch. There were no bombs and no cats. Not much else, either. Besides Ruby's pictures, we were all alone.

Good. Having Father to look after gave me something to live for. And he's a full-time job, I tell you. Between taking him out for walks, tasting his food to make sure it's safe, and watching him watch TV, I barely nap half the day.

I met my new friends Cookie and Bolt. We exchange the latest barks, sniff each other's butts on our walks, and leave messages at the mailbox. I watch for the mailman and let them know so they can bark ahead of time. Cookie's on the lookout for cats, and Bolt keeps track of FedEx since he's faster.

But my first priority is Father. I sleep in his bed to keep him warm, slobber under the table when he eats, and lay my head in his lap to get scratched whenever he smells sad. That helps with my itches and gives him something to do to take his mind off Ruby.

Day after day, I got stronger. Father's smell of loneliness faded.

When fall turned to winter, and snow covered the earth in white magic, I helped him shovel the driveway: I got in his way, bit the shovel, and ate so much snow I had to pee. It was all fun until I remembered playing in the snow with Omar, and my heart filled with longing. I tucked my tail between my legs and curled in the doorway thinking of her.

Father got worried and checked my teeth and my paws. But I wasn't hurt, just sad.

Father understood.

"Oh, Prozak, how I wish I knew what you did all these years. I didn't do much other than mourning Ruby and trying to help other children like her. But you lived a whole life. I know you've been in Afghanistan, but they didn't give me any details. They said they're classified. Like really? That war is over, so what's the harm in telling me what happened to you? Maybe if I asked Walter... Oh well. The past is the past; no point in dwelling on it. We should look to the future."

Still, he seemed preoccupied. I thought he just missed Ruby like I missed Omar, but then he got sneaky. One day I caught him smelling like Walter.

"Like really? You went to see Walter without me?" I growled.

He mumbled something about a Milk-Bone, and I forgot. But he kept acting funny.

He looked at me and smiled for no good reason, so I sniffed him. He smelled like Bolt did every time he buried a bone, so I knew he had a secret. Then he even started going places without me.

"Where are you going? Can I come?" I asked him.

"Just a run to the pharmacy. I won't be long. You stay here; it's too hot for you in the car."

Too hot in the car? In winter?

Hard to believe, but Father was lying to me.

I checked our bed, the kitchen, and even the basement for what he was hiding, but I only found three dirty socks, a dead mouse, and lots of dust.

It was time to be extra vigilant. I followed him to the bathroom every time and supervised him doing his business and brushing his teeth. I followed him from room to room, lay on his phone, and sniffed his privates every morning. Nothing helped.

Then, one day, he brushed me until I crawled under the bed, changed his socks, and brushed his teeth. He turned on the TV to the infomercials and checked his watch.

The doorbell rang.

I barked and ran to the door, as one does. I sniffed, but I couldn't believe my nose.

Father pushed me aside and opened the door. Two women came in, and I knew that my nose had been right.

"Omar? Is this you?"

She kneeled to hug me.

"Sediq! It is you!"

We screamed and barked and laughed and cried.

The other woman wiped her eyes.

"Isn't that wonderful?"

Father sniffed.

"Just as I hoped."

I made a mental note to teach Father proper sniffing technique, then turned back to Omar and wagged my tail so hard it hurt.

"I'm so glad to see you, Omar. How did you find me?"

Omar rubbed my ears but didn't answer. Her dog language still needs work, I thought. I climbed on her lap and licked her nose. She laughed.

The woman talked to Father.

"It wasn't easy, I tell you. Fostering a teenage girl with a single man is not the norm. But girls are not easy to place. Most families want babies, preferably boys. But your outstanding work with disadvantaged children and your impeccable references led the committee to the right decision. I'm delighted. Omar is lucky to have you."

"I'm the lucky one. Omar is an extraordinary kid. I heard the story of their amazing journey across the Afghan mountains. Their courage and loyalty moved me to tears."

He turned to us.

"Welcome home, Omar."

"Thank you. I'm glad to be here with you and Sediq."

I looked at Father.

"What's going on?"

"Omar came to live with us, Prozak," Father said. He smelled truthful, but his recent sneakiness made me weary. I glanced at Omar.

"Really?"

"Really."

I cocked my head.

"Are you sure? We have no cave, you know. Unless you count the basement. As for snow, we have some now, but it always melts in spring. But maybe we could keep some in the freezer..."

Omar laughed.

"Oh, how I missed you, Sediq."

I wagged my tail.

"Me too. But this is awesome. We can play in the snow and go for walks. Here, we walk on sidewalks instead of trails, but don't worry. I'll teach you to sniff the mailboxes and bark at cats. It's safe, since our cats are smaller and they never eat dogs. Father doesn't like it, but we'll only do it when he's on the phone."

I glanced at Father and I had a thought.

"Listen, Omar, how about if you shot us a bear? I know where we can get some salt."

To find out what happened to Prozac's friend Rambo during the the evacuation, read K-9 RAMBO, the Dutch Master:

To learn how bomb dogs are made, check out the first in series, BECOMING K-9, the heartfelt story of a willful pup named Guinness.

AFTERWORD

Thanks for reading K-9 PROZAK. I hope you enjoyed it. If you did, please **take a minute to leave a review,** and tell a friend. That will help others find this book, and I'd appreciate it.

If you haven't already, check out the other books in the **K-9 HEROES** series **BECOMING K-9, BIONIC BUTTER, K-9 VIPER, LOVELY K-9,** and **K-9 PROZAK.**

Go to **RadaJones.com** to sign up for updates, get freebies and stay in touch. I love hearing from you!

Rada

ABOUT THIS BOOK

About this book.

The idea for K-9 Prozak POW was born from two true war dog stories.

The first one was Colonel's story. Colonel was a Belgian Malinois working with the British forces. He was captured in 2014 as his unit tried to drive the Taliban out of the Alingar Valley.

The Taliban's PR video shows Colonel surrounded by five armed Taliban. He looks befuddled. He clearly doesn't understand who these humans are and what they want from him. I wondered how he felt.

The second story is that of dozens of working dogs abandoned in the Kabul airport after the American troop withdrawal. A video shows some of them alongside their new Afghan handlers. The Taliban promised to use them in battle, but neither dogs nor humans looked pleased, and I wonder how that went.So, even if Prozak is a fictional character, the courage and loyalty of working dogs are only too real. I wrote this book as a homage to all the dogs who make our world a better place.

I hope you enjoyed reading K-9 Prozak. If you did, please **take a**

minute to leave a review to introduce other readers to a book they'll enjoy.

To find out what happened to Rambo and meet even more amazing dogs, check out the **K-9 HEROES** series, where the dogs get to tell their stories.

Sign up at **RadaJones.com** to connect and get updates and free-bies. I look forward to hearing from you.

Rada

ABOUT THE AUTHOR

Rada was born in Transylvania, ten miles from Dracula's Castle. Growing up between communists and vampires taught her that humans are fickle, but you can always trust dogs and books. That's why she read every book she could get, including the phone book (too many characters, not enough action), and adopted every stray she found, from dogs to frogs.

After joining her American husband, she spent years studying medicine and working in the ER, but she still speaks like Dracula's cousin.

Rada, her husband Steve, and their dog Guinness live in a cozy Adirondack cabin ruled by a deaf black cat named Paxil. They spend their days writing, hiking, and dreaming about traveling to faraway places.

Go to **RadaJones.com** to sign up for updates and freebies.

facebook.com/RadaJonesMD

twitter.com/JonesRada

instagram.com/RadaJonesMD

bookbub.com/profile/rada-jones

BOOKS BY RADA JONES

BECOMING K-9: A Bomb Dog's Memoir

BIONIC BUTTER: A Three-Pawed K-9 Hero

K-9 VIPER: The Veteran's Story

LOVELY K-9: A Prison Puppy

K-9 RAMBO: The Dutch Master

K-9 PROZAK: POW

MOM: A Dog Story Prequel to BECOMING K-9

K-9 HEROES, Books 1, 2, 3

OVERDOSE: An ER Phycological Thriller

(ER Crimes: The Steele Files Book 1)

MERCY: An ER Thriller

(ER Crimes: The Steele Files Book 2)

POISON: An ER Thriller

(ER Crimes: The Steele Files Book 3)

STAY AWAY FROM MY ER, and Other Fun Bits of Wisdom

ER CRIMES: The Steele Files

Box Set: Books 1-3

EXCERPT FROM MOM
A DOG STORY PREQUEL TO BECOMING K-9

The squirrel dashes, shaking its fluffy tail in a dare, and I take off in hot pursuit. I push the ground away with my hind legs and fly over the thick mossy tree trunk like a bird, slicing the air with my tail as a rudder to give me direction. My front paws touch the ground, and my muzzle ruffles the dry leaves, taking in the musty whiff of mud and mushrooms before I push the dirt away and leap. But my brother Gun's dark shape flies past me like a hawk, and the squirrel screams as my insides twist with pain.

Gun caught it? But we never...

I shake my head to wake up from the dream. I'm no longer a young Alsatian running the forests with my siblings. That was way long ago. These days I'm almost an old lady, and even though my name is Madeline Rose Kahn Van Jones, I prefer to be called Mom.

I curl up in my round bed by Jones's. The nightlight throws silly dark shadows that would be menacing if I didn't know every inch of this place. But I do. It's all familiar - the smell of Dove soap, smoke, and beer. Jones's light snore as he lays on his back. The waxed wooden floors. The full moon glancing through the arched windows.

Somebody yelps in pain again, and I realize that's me. My belly took a life of its own to squeeze, churn, and turn inside out.

Jones sits up and fumbles for his glasses.

"What's up, Maddie? Is it time? I thought we had a few more days!"

He turns on the light, shakes his head to clear it, then grabs his glasses and kneels by my bed. His scent of sweat and care is strangely comforting as he lays gentle, gnarled hands on my stormy belly and gasps.

"Yep. It's time, old girl. Take it easy, sweetheart. You know you can do this. You've done it before."

Sure I did. Five times, in fact. This is my sixth litter, and it hurts, but I'm not afraid. I know it's just a matter of time before my puppies come out, and there's no greater joy. I can't wait to meet them.

Something inside me squeezes again, and I need to push. Jones's hands cup my belly, and his teary eyes pop out as he watches my tail.

"The first one's coming! Push, Maddie, push!"

Like I need you to tell me! I hold my breath and push with all I've got as Jones lifts my tail to look under it.

"Wow, Maddie! You're doing great, but this one's big! Just one more push, baby!"

I push again, but it turns out he lied like humans always do, and nothing happens.

"Just another one, Maddy. You can do that."

I'd like to growl at him to shut up, but I don't have the energy. So I take a deep breath and push like my life depends on it. The pain vanishes, and the pressure releases as #1 pops out.

"Good job, Maddie. There he is."

Jones picks him up and sets him under my nose. I study him carefully. He's just a dark, slippery blob, but he wiggles, and I fall in love. I lick him clean, loving every single inch of him and soothing him as he squeaks like a mouse. He's not much bigger and just half that pretty, but to me, he's the cutest creature in the world. I know he's deaf, blind, and bald, but he's my baby, and that's all that matters.

"Good job, Maddie. This one's gonna be Blue," Jones says, wrapping a tiny blue collar around his neck.

I stick out my tongue to give him a second bath when a terrible cramp takes my breath away.

"There's another one coming," Jones says, staring under my tail.

Thanks for letting me know, I want to growl, but I save my breath to push. A few tries later, #2 pops out.

"This one's gonna be Green. She looks perfect," Jones mutters as he attaches her collar.

I clean her up and inspect every nook and cranny, then proceed to deliver Brown, White, Black, and finally Yellow.

I'm so in love that my heart's about to burst. Jones wipes his eyes with the sleeve of his pajamas before picking them up one by one, studying them, and setting them on my belly. One by one, they sniff their way to crawl to the milk bar, latch on and start feeding.

I'm ecstatic. Exhausted too, but that doesn't matter. All that matters is that they're here, and I love them more than I can say. My whole world is so full of love my heart wants to burst.

Jones pets my head and kisses me. He's flushed and looks prouder than a new dad. His eyes sparkle with joy as he watches them feed.

"Good job, Maddie. You got six, three boys and three girls. They all look healthy and strong."

He brings a bowl of ice water, and I dry it, then I lay on my side to watch the puppies feed. But something suddenly feels wrong. I have to get up and pace, and I must do it now.

I stand, and the puppies fall off the milk bar like ripe fruit. They pile over each other, squeaking. They're mad that dinner is over, but I can't help them right now.

I step away and start pacing.

Jones frowns.

"What's up, Maddie? You ok?"

Buy MOM

www.ingramcontent.com/pod-product-compliance
Lightning Source LLC
Chambersburg PA
CBHW030633190726
48286CB00008B/2504